FAITHFUL FIVE

A Charlie Story

Andrea O'Nan Britton

This book is dedicated to Pam Ritter. Thank you for always taking the time to read my stories and encouraging me to publish them. You are the reason this book is here.
More recently, thank you to Jon Britton, my husband. For staying after me until we finally published.

Love you both.

She has a good life now. It's taken her most of her life to get to the point where she can say to herself, she is truly happy. Her happiness has never been more apparent than in this single moment. She was sitting on the front porch of her modest rural home, swinging in her porch swing, lit by the full moon shining through the slats of her porch. She ran her fingers through the sweaty curly blond hair of her little boy. As she twisted a curl around her pointer finger, she felt the sweet five years old, who had his head in her lap, wiggle slightly. She hated to leave this peaceful moment, no city lights, no passing cars, nothing to disturb the crickets singing their songs as they labor through the night. In the distance, she could hear the bullfrogs in the lake burping their deep melody. The crickets and bullfrogs chorused together as if in a choir singing a song to nature. However, she thought it best to get her son in his bed before he completely woke up.

She drew her son close to her chest and rocked the porch swing a few more times before finally lifting herself with her son cradled in her arms. The house was dark, and she had only left a single light burning in the tiny hall between their two bedrooms. She made her way through the dark house slowly and into her son's room. She carefully laid the sleeping boy in his big boy bed and covered him with a light blanket. She bent down over him and placed a gentle kiss on the top of his sweaty little head. As she left the room, she looked back to enjoy and appreciate the sight one last time for the day.

She turned out the hall light and switched on the lamp next to the couch. Climbing onto the couch and settling in with her favorite blanket, while reaching for her book she had left on the coffee table. She truly enjoyed these peaceful quiet moments. So much of her young adult life had been so hectic and full of unnecessary noise. Sometimes, she thought about her childhood, a nurturing, peaceful one, and wondered how she went from a wonderful childhood to chaotic young adult life. Thinking about her past didn't make her sad or angry it only made her appreciate how far she had come.

She must have fallen asleep at some point because a tapping sound at the door awakened her. At first, she thought she was dreaming. She rarely had visitors way out in the rural part of the county where her cabin is located. Especially an uninvited visitor. The whole reason she bought the place out in the sticks was to maintain a quiet life for her and her son.

As the tapping brought her to attention and out of the fog of sleep, she began to realize it wasn't a dream. When she looked at the window next to the door, she saw a figure standing there. She could only see a shadow from the full moon shinning against the person, but there was definitely someone there. Whoever was at the door was very persistent and continuing to tap on the door and then the window and then back to the door. The longer the tapping went on, the more nervousness built up inside her. Before anxiety totally took over, she stood to her feet. She realized the visitor at the door must see her shadow moving inside the room because the tapping stopped.

She started towards the door then stopped; thinking better of her decision, she turned to the small table next to her couch, pulled the small draw open, and reached inside. She pulled out a small handgun. The hard, cool metal in her hand brought her to fully awake. She held it for a moment, looking at it. Then, she checked the chamber with her back to the door and then pulled the level back to load the gun. She slid the small gun in the back pocket of her jeans and walked to the door. She placed her hand on the gun in her back pocket and looked through the window by the door.

She recognized the uninvited visitor, but that did little to settle her nerves. Thoughts were darting through her mind like bumblebees swarming a nice fresh patch of honeysuckle. Her sleepy blue eyes peered through the window. The visitor motioned to her through the window for her to open the door. She shook her head no, the concern of his presence growing inside her. She recognized the man on the porch, but he looked different. His usually neat and tidy hair was long, too long, and messy like he had ridden in a car with the windows down. It was greasy looking and tangled. His face had an overgrown beard, which was typically kept nice and clean-shaven. Although he wasn't normally a sharp dresser, his clothes were usually clean, pressed, and newer looking. Now, standing on her porch, his tee-shirt looked dirty and had several rips long the neck hem. It was wrinkled and faded. His jeans looked dirty at the knees and had ink or oil stains along the pockets. His bare feet were dirty like he'd walked from the road to her house, but she could see his truck sitting in her driveway. She was confused; where were his shoes. More importantly, why was he here? It seemed like such a long time since she had seen him.

Standing on the porch, he placed his hands in the universal sign for prayer and mouthed the words 'please open the door.' Still hesitant, she rolled her eyes, shaking her head no more vigorously now, and stepped away from the window. She pulled her fingers through her long dark brown hair and took a deep breath. Her straight, tangled hair fell right back down into her face. She pulled a hair tie off her wrist. In one swift motion, she twisted her hair up into a bun. She walked to the door and slid the chain lock into the locked position so he could not open the door all the way, but she could crack the door and speak to him.

She turned the lock on the doorknob and twisted the deadbolt to unlock it. As she heard the deadbolt click and unlock, a nervous shock wave pulsed through her entire body. She pulled the door open and pushed her face into the crack, and asked, "What are you doing here?"

He exhaled and smiled and pushed his hands deep into his pockets. "Please, will you let me in? I really want to talk to you." He said in a humbled innocent voice.

She took a step back and shook her head no, "I can't let you in, I'm sorry. My son is asleep, and it's too late to have people in the house right now."

His smile and his innocent puppy dog eyes fell. The disappointment was showing clearly in his eyes. He started to explain, "I drove all the way out here to see you."

When she interrupted, "Well, you shouldn't have."

His eyes began to reflect less disappointment and began to turn to anger. Still Shaking her head no, Charlie closed the door. Before she could lock the deadbolt, the uninvited visitor kicked the door with the full force of a flat foot. The door flew open hard, breaking the chain lock. The door hit her in the face and knocked her backward with a thud. Dazed momentarily, she sat still on the floor. He pushed his way in, yelling "Bitch" through clenched teeth. "This isn't the way I wanted this to go."

He grabbed her hair to pull her to her feet. As she tried to gain footing, she remembered her son sleeping in the next room and willed herself not to scream. She reached behind her into her back pocket and wrapped her fingers tightly around the weapon. She swung the armed gun in a roundhouse style swing and hit the man with the butt of the gun on the cheek, splitting it open. He released her hair.

Her bun was limp and falling to one side. She pulled the weapon around to the front of her and aimed. Before she could squeeze off a shot, the visitor, with full force, lunged at her, catching her just below her knees. She hit the ground hard; the gun flew from her grip and slid across the hardwood floor, landing under the table.

She heard the visitor say in a sugary, overly sweet tone, "Hey buddy. Mommy fell. Let's get you back to bed."

She knew he was talking to her son. She frantically searched for the gun on her hands and knees. She heard him shut her son's bedroom door then slide something in front of the door so he couldn't get out of his room. When the man returned, he stood momentarily watching her frantically searching for her weapon. Hate, greed, and anger covered his face as she watched him slowly bend down and pick up her gun from under the table beside the couch. Without a word, the visitor walked to her. She turned over to her back and brought her feet up. She kicked him as hard as she could with both feet in the chest.

Temporarily, knocking the breath from him. Seeing the man was struggling for breath, she took the opportunity to stand and get another blow in. With everything in her, knowing she must protect her son, she punched him in the nose. The man's eyes immediately filled with water and his nose began to bleed. She lifted her leg and kicked him in the chest. She began to claw at his face and arms as he was slowly making his comeback. With her own gun, he hit her on the side of the head and grabbed at her neck, and pulled her to the floor. Flailing her arms and legs as he pulled her back, she made contact with his face again, but this did not slow him down. Her efforts to regain control did little compared to his strength. He threw her to the floor, then straddling her, began to choke her with his hands around her neck. She slapped his face and clawed her fingernails into his cheeks. As he continued to choke her, she clawed at his hands and ran her fingernails down his arms, leaving long deep cuts in his skin. Just before she lost consciousness, the man lifted her head and slammed it hard on the floor, then stood and looked down at her. The man stepped away from her for a moment. Without slowing or stopping his pace, he walked directly to her and stomped his barefoot in her face.

18 Years Earlier

At age 9, charlotte, her two older brothers, and her younger sister moved to the small town of Harriston. Harriston, located about 30 minutes outside of Center City, which was the largest city around, the small community. However, Harriston was growing with industrial factories moving in from the bigger city. Because there wasn't enough land to build the large factories in the city, Harriston was close enough to the city to commute and had the acreage for the factories. Charlotte's parents had decided they wanted their children to attend a smaller school than what the larger city could provide and began speaking to the community of Harriston about funding a Christian school. It didn't take long to find several families interested in the idea. As the local families pitched the idea to the local churches, a plan for a Christian school funded by surrounding churches began to form.

At age 10, Charlotte sat uncomfortably in her itchy lace dress in the First Baptist church's sanctuary, where they were holding an open call for families wanting to sign their children up for the Christian school. Charlotte and her siblings already knew they would be attending in the fall. Her Mother told her that she should be excited to see what other children her age would be attending the school. However, Charlotte was not excited, not at all. All she could think about was the dress scratching her neck, and she wanted so badly to get to the playground and swing upside down on the monkey bars.

Towards the end of the night, she heard the pastor closing the meeting, saying, "So talk this over with your family, and if you decide you want your children to attend, you will need to bring all paperwork to our final enrollment meeting next Saturday." Charlotte was relieved to hear the words coming from the pastor because that meant she would be able to leave the sanctuary, which she did, and head right to the playground, which she did.
Charlotte hung upside down by her knees, her dress flipped over, almost covering her face. She could hear her Mother's pleasantly sweet laughter floating out the door of the big first Baptist church building. As her parents exited, she swung around to see them, still hanging upside down; she called to them, "Hey momma, daddy!"

Both her parents turned to see her hanging there. When her Mother called out, "Charlotte Rae Ann, get down from there."

The warm summer air from the end of a hot summer day caused her hands to be moist with sweat, but she did as she was told and swung down to the ground. Both feet hit the ground with a thud, and she bolted towards her parents. Her younger sister clung to her Mother's leg like a toad on a lily pad.

"Don't worry, momma, no one is here; no one can see my under panties." Charlotte said as she approached her parents.

The group of couples giggled under their breath, and Charlotte's dad, with a smile, said, "Well, Charlie Rae, we are here now, and we could see your undergarments."

Charlotte agreed sweetly and, without a second thought, began to walk towards their car. Her parents quickly said their goodbyes and broke away from the group, and loaded into their vehicle.

Charlotte and her family lived on a little farm in the rural area of Harriston. They didn't really farm the land, but they kept a few cows to keep the fields from becoming overgrown. They had a few chickens, a billy goat, and a few dogs. Charlotte had a great life on the little farm. No one that saw the little girl's sweet feminine angel face would ever imagine a fierce warrior was hiding there inside her. The week before the school orientation Charlotte lived her best summer life. She crept from her warm bed early every morning, slid on her muck boots, and headed to the creek, usually with her older brother. She would run the fields, climb the trees, hunt for crawl dads and snakes. She would flip rocks, throw rocks, make mud pies and fight epic imaginary battles. Charlotte would play till sundown, then run home with her brother, eat dinner, bathe and fall asleep wherever she sat still for longer than 30 seconds. The next day she would wake up in her bed and do it all over again. Occasionally Charlotte's parents saw her from a distance, walking through the field with a stick in one hand, in her shorts and mud boots. They wondered what went on in her little mind but never questioned her.

The evening of the orientation, Charlotte's Mother called her in early from playing; this was not ideal for Charlotte. She had cornered the biggest crawdad she had ever seen. Now, she had to leave it and try to recapture it again later. Charlie immediately became cross with her parents. Her foul mood continued as they entered the building where the new school would be housed. The school would be one large room with chairs in the middle for meetings, and there would be makeshift walls along the sides of the large room's outer walls to make classrooms. The large room was a former gymnasium, and so every little noise echoed through the room. It had its limitations, but all the families involved were satisfied and believed it would be a great start.

Charlotte and her family entered the large room smiling. Well, everyone but charlotte. Charlotte had on another fluffy dress, white socks with lace on the ends, and white Mary Janes. She hated it. She would never admit that it wasn't as itchy as the other lace dress but still hated it all the same. She slowly walked behind her father, arms crossed and head down. She was wearing an angry frown, and there was no mistaking from anyone that saw Charlotte or Miss. Charlie Rae, as her dad called her, she was not happy to be there. She and her family took a seat on the third row of chairs in the meeting area. Her Mother and father waved and said hello to families as they arrived, and soon the pastor took his place at the front of the room and began the orientation.

Once the pastor had finally finished welcoming the crowd, he asked that all the children break into groups and head to their classrooms so they could meet their teachers and talk to what would be their new classmates. Charlotte sulked to where her new classroom would be and took a seat, arms still crossed without saying a word to her family. She sat staring at the floor and kicking imaginary dirt with her new white Mary Janes. She was the only one in there at the moment, until a boy her age entered the class. Without raising her head, Charlotte lifted her eyes to look at the boy. He nodded his head to her as if to say hello. Charlotte did a half fake smile and continued looking at the floor. Charlotte waited for what seemed like the eternity of her life. More people entered the makeshift room, but none of them interested her. Once everyone had come in and settled down, the class teacher stood at the head of the classroom and welcomed the children and their parents. Charlotte looked up for the first time to see everyone in her class. All the children in the room were boys. When the teacher asked if any of the children had a question, Charlotte raised her hand shyly. When the teacher called on her, she cleared her throat and quietly asked, "Where's the other girls?" The teacher, not exactly sure how to answer, told her, "Well, for now, you are the only girl." Charlotte nodded her head and mouthed "oh" more to herself than to the teacher.

When the teacher released the class, Charlotte headed to the field at the back of the building. A small playground had been set up for the children. Charlotte was ill over the whole situation. All she could think was she would never have a friend now, and she would never have someone to play with. Boys were gross, and she didn't want to talk to them, much less play with them. She twisted herself on the swing and dragged her new white Mary Janes through the dirt and dust. Charlotte was in the middle of an angry thought and kicking the ground when she heard footsteps approaching and then a voice "Hey there." She looked up, a little shocked to see someone talking to her. A boy her age, one of the boys from the classroom, was standing in front of her. She said, "Hey," back and dropped her head again and continued to drag her feet. Her long fine brown hair fell into her face.

The boy took a seat on the swing next to her and continued, "My name is Farmer. what's your name?"

Charlotte stopped twisting in the swing and answered, "Charlie."

Farmer said, "I guess we are going to be in class together."

Charlotte didn't answer. She just nodded her head. Farmer was of average height for his age, with dark hair and brown eyes. His skin was tanned from playing outside. He played sports, and though his muscle tone hadn't developed yet, it was apparent that he was athletically gifted. A few minutes later, two more boys walked over from the school building and introduced themselves as James and Roger. James and Roger were both painfully thin. They may have liked to watch basketball or football, but they didn't play, not well anyway. They had the build of book nerds, which Charlotte would later find out, is precisely what they were. Both tall and lanky, both determined to be the head of the class, and both were very capable. That's where the similarities ended. James had blond hair and blue eyes, where Roger had black hair and brown eyes. James had a perfect toothy smile, whereas Roger had a huge smile full of teeth, but none seemed to be where they were supposed to be. Although both looked out of place in their skin at times, they were both still handsome in their way.

Three more boys were playing out in the field behind the playground. Farmer explained that their names were Aaron, Vincent and Sam. Aaron and Sam were brothers, only about a year and a half apart. Both had dirty blond hair and blue eyes. Sam, the older of the two, was thick and never really seemed to hurry for much. Aaron was short for his age but thin with muscular legs. Both boys obviously worked as farmhands with someone. Aaron and Vincent were best friends. Vincent seemed out of place with this group. He was very tall, taller than the other boys, and he was very thin. He had long blond hair and greenish-brown eyes. Charlotte later learned Vincent was very artistic and played a lot of soccer. His family wasn't from Harriston. Once Charlotte got to know the boys better, she realized Vin actually fit in quite well.
Charlotte asked if they all were going to be in a class together too. Farmer explained that He and Sam were a year older and were going in the 5th grade. They were the only 5th graders enrolled, so they would be in her class with the other boys.

The sun was starting to set over the field. Charlotte looked out towards the trees at the back of the field. From where they were, it looked like a snake was hanging from one of the trees. Just as Charlotte had made her mind up that it was a snake, not a low hanging branch

Roger said, "Looks like a snake is hangin from that tree over there."

Charlotte said, "I know. I'm going to go look at it."

She jumped from her swing and took off running towards the trees. The boys looked at one another, shrugged their shoulders, and took off after her yelling "Charlie, wait up!"

The group of kids running towards the trees caught the attention of the other three boys playing in the field, and they began to head towards Charlie and the others to see what was going on. Once Charlie reached the tree, she wasted no time and began to climb the tree which housed the snake. Sam was the last to arrive at the group surrounding the tree. He wasn't overweight, but he also wasn't thin. He just chose not to be bothered with acting like he cared as much as the other boys.

One of the boys on the ground yelled up at Charlie, "Is it a snake for sure?"

Charlotte whispered down to the boys, "Yeah, for sure, it's a cow sucker."

Cow suckers were common in this area of the south. They aren't shy, and they get their name because of the myth that they will drink the milk of a cow straight from its utters if the utters are full enough. Cow Suckers, also known as rat snakes, are thick black, and very long. Their head is almost as large as an adult's hand. This is why the boys all agreed loudly that it was cool and asked if she could get it down. Charlie agreed and told them she was trying. Just as Charlie reached out alongside the branch to grab the snake's head, she lost her footing and slid from the tree. She fell hard to the ground and landed on her back. Her dress was up over her face, and her long skinny legs sprawled out. The boys rushed to Charlie's side and kneeled next to her. They all asked, concerned if she was alright. Charlie wiped the dress from her face, and catching her breath; she began to laugh. Through tears of laughter, she said, "Oh my gosh did you see that! I almost had it!"

James and Roger stood up and reached down for Charlie's hands to help her up.

Sam shook his head and said, "Damn girl, you are crazy."

Charlotte just shrugged. "So. Not being crazy is not fun."

"I'm Sam. I hear we are gonna be in class together."

"Yeah, that's what I hear." Charlotte said

Sam just smiled with a mouth full of braces and shook his head again.

About that time, Charlotte could hear her dad calling for her.

"That's my dad. I guess I should go." Charlotte said, dusting off her dress.

The boys bid her goodbye, and Sam and Farmer said in unison, "See ya in a week."

Charlotte waved back at them and said, "See ya," and ran towards the family car.

Little did Charlotte know that meeting her new classmates that night would change her life forever. Not just change her life but change her whole life's path for the future.

As she loaded into her family's car, she thought to herself maybe she could be friends with those boys after all.

Present-Aaron

When Charlotte first met Aaron, he was short for his age and didn't hit his true growth potential until college. He was brilliant, but his intelligence wasn't measured the way most teachers measure intelligent kids. Throughout school, Aaron masked his intelligence with meaningless comments and witty phrases that normally disrupted the class. He later attended college on a scholarship and obtained a master's degree in chemical engineering. From the day Aaron graduated high school, his college experience was a battle. He did not have an easy childhood. Those struggles followed him throughout most of his life.

Aaron's mother still lived in Harriston, although Aaron had moved to the city limits after college to continue his career. His house on a small piece of land was close to Harriston but closer to Center City, making for an easy commute. For the last two years, Aaron had been coming home on the weekends to spend time with his Mother and keep himself busy and out of trouble. The weekend trips were good for him and better for his Mother. He was able to help maintain their old farmhouse and keep her company. Although his Mother wore on his nerves most of the time, he was happy to be there for her and realized the benefit was for both of them.

When Aaron was a sophomore in high school and Sam a junior, their father was killed in a tragic car accident. He'd been driving drunk and ran his car into a tree. He was killed instantly. Their Mother, concerned about raising the boys alone and about being able to afford to raise the boys alone, quickly re-married and had two more sons with her new husband. When the younger boys were in middle school, their father left with no explanation, which left Aaron and Sam to help their Mother raise the younger boys and work as farmhands to help provide for their family. None of them had an easy life, but they made it. All the boys had successfully made a good life for themselves. Or at least it had seemed so from the outside looking in.

Aaron navigated his car into the long gravel driveway that led to his Mother's old farmhouse. The large two-story, wooden slated house was white. Paint chipped and sunburned, it was still a beautiful sight with its wrap-around porch and hanging baskets. Although the house was on a slow decline, Aaron and his mother worked hard to keep looking like a show house. Aaron's mother, now retired, always had a list of projects for Aaron to start on. Aaron didn't mind. He liked helping, and he enjoyed staying busy. His brothers rarely visited, but occasionally they would come for Sunday dinner, which pleased his mother.

Aaron parked his car, grabbed the groceries he'd bought, and headed to the back of the house. His arms full of bags; he slung the screen door open with a pinky finger and steadied the door with a foot so he could maneuver his way into the house. Once in the house, he found his mother in the kitchen. She rushed to his aid to help with the arm full of bags. They said their hellos and hugged. Although he would never admit it, Aaron thought the hugs and attention he got from his Mother were probably why he continued to come every weekend. Aaron and his Mother busily worked around the kitchen and talked about their week. He told his Mother about work and what he'd been doing all week. His mother told him stories she'd heard and caught him up on the town gossip. Aaron mentally rolled his eyes over the gossip. He didn't really want to know all the towns made up stories, but it made his Mother feel better to share something, anything with him.

It was Friday night. As they discussed their plans for Saturday, Aaron grabbed a soda can from the refrigerator and popped it open. The can made the unmistakable air pressure release noise. His Mother hearing the noise, whipped her head around and went to grab the can from Aaron. Aaron jerked the can back away from her.

"Mom! It's soda." He said indefinitely.

His Mother paused and took a deep breath. "I'm sorry, it's a habit." She explained, "they die hard, you know."

"I know, but I'm not drinking, and I have no intentions of going back to that. I know you have heard it before, but I am determined this time." Aaron explained.

"Now, if we can get Sam to follow your lead." His Mother said

Aaron frowned. "You know Sam isn't speaking to me right now." He stated with his head lowered, picking at the tab on the soda can.

They graciously let the moment pass and continued their task at hand.

For years Aaron's Mother had been the voice of reason as she watched her boys make mistake after mistake with alcohol and drugs. The younger boys had followed, the older boys lead but had quickly recovered when they were a year or so out of college. However, alcoholism ran deep in the older boy's father, and it took longer for them. Aaron had been sober for two years and was determined to lead the family away from this disease. The younger boys were on board, but Sam, the oldest, couldn't understand the issue. He had a job, a house, a car and was supposedly happy. In turn, this caused a ripple between Aaron and Sam.

An hour or so later, Aaron and his Mother took their drinks to the back porch to watch the sunset. The day was beginning to cool, and the sun was setting behind the hills at the back of the property. They sat in silence as the sky painted a beautiful summer portrait.

His mother broke the silence. "You and Charlie have spent some time together, lately, haven't you?" she asked.

"Yeah, she lives just over the hill; it makes it easier to see her. She's been a big help through this recovery process." Aaron answered

"Did you hear what happened?" his mother said, still looking to the sky.

Aaron answered "No," almost nonresponsive expecting the news to be more gossip from town.

"She's in the hospital. She may not make it." His Mother said, now looking to Aaron.

Aaron jerked his head to his mother. "What! Why didn't you tell me sooner?"

"She was attacked in her home last night." His Mother explained

Aaron dropped his drink and jumped up, "What do you mean? Is Ryan alright? Which hospital?" Aaron had a million questions, and his Mother had no answers.

"Her son, Ryan, is fine. She is at Harriston Memorial hospital." His Mother said anxiously, "I didn't think you would be so upset. Where are you going?"

Aaron jerked the door open to the house and reemerged with his keys. "I have to go see her."

"Aaron, slow down; I'm sure you can't get in to see her right now. It's late." His mother said, trying to be the voice of reason as always.

Aaron looked at his watch and began to take a few breaths. "I'm Gonna call the guys."

He went back into the house to look for his phone. His first call was going to be to Vincent, his best friend all through school. He was scrolling through his phone to look for Vincent's phone number when his mind took him to a memory of Charlie. He'd been so grateful for her willingness to talk to him when he was feeling depressed. She'd spent time with him when he felt he wanted to drink. Or even work alongside him when he needed to stay busy and keep his mind off his current situations. But these weren't the memories that came to him now. His mind drifted back to when he was a teenager and the death of his father. Charlie had been the one to go to his side after everyone was leaving the funeral home. She sat with him in silence support and let him cry privately. Charlie never judged him, or Sam and she always tried to give words of wisdom. However, this time she just sat with him and let him work out whatever emotions he felt.

Once he had gained composure, she looked at him and took his hand.

"Want to go hang upside down in that tree like we did when we were 12?" she asked

Aaron, expecting her to try to give words of wisdom or some kind of Charlie comfort, was taken aback by the suggestion. He looked past her at the tree and then smiled.

"Yeah, actually I do." He answered

They stood up and slowly walked to the enormous oak tree on the side of the funeral home. Charlie climbed the tree first, then Aaron followed. Working themselves around, they finally flipped over and were hanging there upside down, arms flailing weightlessly. They looked at each other and started to laugh. Charlie's shirt remained safely tucked into her jeans, but her hair was hanging and slightly drifting from side to side in the wind. Her eyes still sad, but her mouth is turned in a smile. Aaron's heat-wilted tie was flipped over and rubbing his cheek; his shirt had come untucked and was showing a small triangle of his belly. People leaving the funeral home saw them and not sure whether to laugh or be offended to see two teenagers hanging upside down in a tree at a funeral just walked past without comment. They couldn't hang there as long as they did when they were children and soon flipped back up. They sat on the tree branch. Charlie looked at Aaron, "It's all going to be alright. We just have to keep enjoying the small moments when we can."

Aaron grabbed Charlie's hand and squeezed as he nodded his head in agreement.

The memory brought a smile to Aaron's mouth, but his eyes still shown concern as he picked the number for Vincent on his phone and pressed the call button.

Present-Vincent

Vincent, originally from the California area, moved down south with his parents around age 5. His parents lasted a couple of years after the move and divorced when he was about to turn 9. His father moved from Harriston back to Center City, and his Mother stayed in Harriston with Vincent. Vincent was not a very happy child. He blamed his mother for the divorce and always wanted his father. Vincent's father was always traveling and rarely saw his son. But in Vincent's mind, as a child, he only saw his Mother as the obstacle keeping him from his father. Vincent threw himself into self-expression with displays of art, music, and sculpting. He was a talented artist and could draw anything anyone wanted him to. Had it not been for his love of art and his way of escaping, he would have been a much more troubled child. His mother knew this and let him use the talents he possessed as a way out of his head. Although at times his art seemed dark and troubled her, she was just open-minded enough to know that he needed this outlet to release his anger.

After high school, Vincent attended art school in New York but returned south with a pregnant wife after college. He didn't move to Harriston but Center City, just outside of Harriston, where he began sculpting and tried opening an interactive art gallery. It wasn't until after his first child was born that he realized he'd been harsh in his treatment of his Mother. When his son was born, he craved holding him and smelling his head. He and his wife were having marital trouble, but that never stopped him from wanting to see his son and spending as much time as possible with him. This realization brought Vincent to the reality that his father was the selfish perpetrator in his parents' marriage.

Nonetheless, his father's relationship grew due to the nature of their common business practices, and he made a purposeful effort to keep his Mother involved in his life and his child's life. The rough areas of his marriage were smoothed out, and eventually, they had a second child. The family was making it work. Before the birth of their second child, his interactive gallery was failing, and ultimately once that ended, his marriage was less stressed. Due to the cultured scene around the city, Vincent opened another gallery where local and out of town or out-of-state artists could display their work. He even included a second-floor gallery for young artists to display their work and an after-hours basement gallery that served appetizers and beverages. Had Vincent not come to the tough decision to close the interactive gallery, he would have never been able to see the future in his new venture. It took him years to obtain the multi-level gallery, but it had been completed about two years ago with the basement level and had been turning a profit since its conception.

Currently, Vincent lived on the 4th floor of the gallery with his wife, Ella, son, Duke, and daughter, Pixie. The 4th floor also held his studio, where he developed and created all his masterpieces. At the moment, Vin was finishing up a canvas piece and could hear his wife and children in the kitchen cooking dinner. He had the windows of the studio cracked to let in the warm summer air. In the summer, he loved to hear the commotion as people carried on their lives right below his windows.

Just as he was about to leave the studio to join his family for dinner, he heard his phone chirp to life. Looking for the phone under papers and paint-covered towels, he found it in his pants pocket. He checked the display screen, and it read "Aaron the Amazing." Seeing his longtime friend from school's name pop up on the screen brought a smile to his face. He punched the answer button and said, "Hey Aaron, what's up man, been a while."

Aaron had always referred to Vincent as Vin, and Vin could tell by the tone in Aaron's voice immediately that this call would not be a simple check-up call. Something was going on.

As Vin listened to Aaron explain the situation, his heart fell to his stomach. He was speechless; all he could muster was a "yes" or "I understand." His wife, Ella, came to the doorway to the studio to announce dinner was ready, but when she saw Vin's face, she didn't speak. Immediately she could tell something was wrong. Vin looked his wife in the eyes and shook his head. Ella left the doorway and crossed the room to be by Vin's side. She didn't know what was going on, but she knew something must be seriously wrong.

Aaron explained he was going to go to the hospital first thing in the morning. Although Vin lived about an hour from the hospital, he insisted on meeting Aaron there. He said he could be there around 12. Vin explained that he had Farmer write up some contracts for the studio a few months back, so he would call Farmer and let him know what's happened. Vin thought that Farmer would also have James and Roger's contact information. James and Farmer worked on a lot of projects together. Aaron thanked Vin and told him he couldn't function at total capacity right now. Vin was happy to do it.

When the call to Aaron was disconnected, he turned to his wife with tears in his eyes. She leaned in and hugged him.

"Vin, what's going on?" she asked with complete concern.

Vincent explained the situation about Charlie and told her he had to go for a few days. Not just to see Charlie, but he had to be there for Aaron. He was concerned about Aaron's drinking and didn't know how this would affect his frame of mind. Ella completely supported Vincent's decision and agreed; he had to support his friends. Ella was an interior decorator and helped run the gallery alongside Vincent. She was perfectly capable of handling things while Vincent was gone. He trusted her completely and knew there was no one better to fill in for him.

That night Vincent lay awake in bed next to Ella. Ella's head rested firmly on his chest. She stirred a little and then asked, "What's on your mind, my love."

Vincent breathed in heavily and released the weight of the world from his body.

He said, "You know, Charlie was a force to be reckoned with back in the day. I can't imagine her being any less now. You know if it weren't for Charlie, you and I may not be here now."

"Really, what do you mean?" Ella asked curiously

"Well, back when we were having trouble, right after Duke was born, I ran into Charlie at a Gallery outside Chicago. We had lunch, and I was telling her about Duke and us. She is the one that encouraged me to give up the interactive gallery to save our marriage." He said, pressing his chin to his chest to try to get a look at his wife, still lying on his chest.

"I didn't know that. Now that you mention it, when you came back from Chicago, you were different and a lot more determined." She said with a smile remembering her husband's take-charge attitude. She ran a finger down her husband's chest. "Well, she certainly deserves your thanks then, and so do I." Ella said with a smile

"I know, if it weren't for us working out our differences, we wouldn't have Pixie," Vincent said, thinking of their daughter toddling around the house in her lime green ballet skirt and a princess crown. They both lay there quietly with heavy hearts and minds until they eventually fell asleep.

The following day, as soon as Vincent woke up, he grabbed his phone and searched for Farmer's contact information.

Present-Farmer

Otis Wendall Farmer, more commonly known as Farmer, is named after his father, grandfather, and great-grandfather. When he was born, his mother didn't have a choice in his name. However, she did choose Wendall which, in his opinion, was just as horrible as Otis. As soon as he was old enough to talk, he voiced his disdain for his name. On the first day of Kindergarten, he introduced himself as Farmer, and it stuck. Most of his friends in public school didn't know his given first name. When he started in 5th grade at the private school, he continued his introductions as Farmer, hoping that again no one would realize Farmer wasn't his given name. However, all hope was lost when the principal insisted on calling everyone by their formal name, Mr. Farmer. Charlie once asked why he was Mr. Farmer, and she couldn't be Ms. Charlotte. When the principal told her his last name was Farmer, the class realized his given name wasn't Farmer Farmer. The class insisted on Farmer telling his "real name" for weeks until finally he gave in and told them his name was Otis, and he better never hear them call him that. Occasionally, his mother and father would call him Dale, short for Wendall, but mostly everyone called him Farmer.

Farmer was athletic and excelled in school as well. When their private school started, there were only two fifth graders, Farmer and Aaron's brother Sam. Students came and would stay a year or a few years over the years. Still, Farmer was the only original student to graduate the private school 12th-grade graduation. After graduation, Farmer began community college. He attended the community college for a year before being offered a scholarship to one of the state's major business colleges. He graduated with a bachelor's in business. After college graduation, he immediately started his own business management company in Harriston. There was nothing like this type of business in Harriston, so he was very successful, mostly because he was very good at his job.

Despite his success, his personal life was slowly starting to deteriorate. After college, he married and brought his young wife back to Harriston. They tried for years to conceive a child but were unable. After coming to terms with the fact that they would not have children, they began marriage counseling to rebuild their relationship. Two years of counseling produced no success. One night Farmer came home from work to find an empty house. His wife had left without warning and refused to speak with Farmer over the phone, email, or in person. Approximately three weeks after she left, Farmer received divorce papers in the mail. After conferring with his pastor and family, he signed them and returned them. His divorce had been final for about two years now, and he'd been on a few dates friends set him up with, but ultimately he wasn't interested in a relationship or in being remarried. So, he threw himself into work and continued to excel.

Farmer sat on his front porch watching the sunrise in his pajama pants and a sleep-soaked tee shirt. He sipped his coffee and let his mind wander freely. It was Saturday, so work and business at hand was the last thing on his mind. He thought about showering and heading into town to roam the local hardware store. Maybe he would surf the internet and find a new project. He looked down at the papers that had fallen to his feet and focused specifically on one page. It was a foster parent application for adoption. He'd been at unease lately in his free time. He'd set his business up so well, and most of the time, he didn't need to focus on the business, just maintain the business relationships he'd already created. He was capable of caring for a child both in physical time and monetarily. His family was supportive of the idea, so he didn't know why he hesitated to proceed.

He lifted himself from the rocking chair and walked into the house just as his cell phone started to buzz. Cursing to himself about not working on a Saturday, he answered harshly.

The voice on the other end said, "Farmer? Hey, it's Vin."

Farmer tried to refocus his mind from work to the current phone call and stumbled over his words, "Hey, what, what are you doing?"

Farmer listened as Vin explained. Farmer insisted on meeting Vin and Aaron at the hospital at noon. He told Vin he would contact Roger and James. Before Vin could hang up Farmer interrupted, "has anyone contacted Sam?"

There was a slight pause on Vincent's end, "No. He and Aaron aren't talking right now. And he's been on a bender. We didn't know if it was a good idea to involve him."

Farmer dropped his head and closed his eyes tight. He was thinking to himself, "Oh Sam, not again." But didn't voice his thoughts to Vin. "OK, probably best not to then." He said.

They disconnected, and without wasting any time, Farmer pulled up James' phone number.

Present-James and Roger

All through school, James and Roger had a healthy competition as to who would be their class's valedictorian. Nether would hold ill will towards the other, but they did spur each other to do their better than best. Neither was very athletically gifted, but they both played basketball for the school. Most boys at the school did because there wasn't much else to do at that time. At the end of their senior year, James pulled out on top but only by a half-point or so.

James went on to college on a full scholarship and, after college, continued to law school. After law school, he took a job in the city for a large law firm, where he exceeded greatly but felt he wasn't helping people directly as he had originally intended to do. By this time, he'd married and had two little girls. He moved his family back to Harriston and opened a firm with a coworker from his previous employer. Shortly after the move, he and his wife had a boy and then another little girl. Although his firm didn't bring in as much money as his previous job, he was more satisfied. The business flourished, and both partners were delighted with the result of the risk they had taken.

Roger had done very well for himself as well. He attended college directly out of high school and obtained a bachelor's in science. He and his girlfriend at the time had found themselves expecting, so he left college, married, and had a beautiful baby boy. A few years later, Roger decided to return to college to complete his science degree, where he ended with a doctorate in molecular science. He taught college for a few years, and after the birth of their second son, he was hired by some big corporation to develop some secret jet fuel.

No one knows what Roger does, but it provides a good life for him and his family. No one wanted to ask what Roger's job was because his explanation would only prove to make the interested individual feel stupid no matter how intelligent they were.

This morning it so happened that James and Roger had their monthly breakfast meeting and golf outing. The two had truly found a friendship in one another all those years ago, and they felt blessed to have found it. James laughed his big toothy smile as he talked to Roger about a strange request a client had proposed. Roger smiled a perfectly toothed smile. He was proud of his expensive smile, which was the first thing he afforded when he could. They were mid-laugh when James' phone began to vibrate on the table. Looking at the screen, James said, "well, speak of the devil." Through grinning teeth.

Roger continued to shovel eggs and potatoes in his mouth while James answered the phone. Roger was thinking about how he could fit in a couple of extra miles running to burn off his breakfast calories when he noticed James' face fell and the smile that previously lit up his face faded. Roger knew the call wasn't good news. He could hear James agreeing to something, say ing 'they would meet them at the hospital.' Roger assumed it meant He and James would meet Farmer at the hospital.

When James disconnected, he didn't leave time for Roger to ask questions.

"Well, we are going to have to forego the golf today."

Roger looking at James curiously, said, "Ok, you gonna tell me why."

James looked at Roger, his face sullen, "It's Charlie."

Roger dropped his fork and wiped his lips with the cloth napkin, "What's going on?"

The clubhouse was noisy as James explained, "She was attacked last night in her house. It's serious. They don't know what happened." James said and, taking a deep breath, finished, "Ryan was there when it happened, but he is alright. The details are very vague."

 Roger ran his hands through his goatee, "Damn, this isn't good."

James pressed his lips together and shook his head, "no, no, it isn't. We are meeting the guys at the hospital at noon."

Roger agreed. As they finished their breakfast, Roger said, "Remember that time we went hiking in Bluffton Falls park?"

James smiled as he took a drink of water, "I was just thinking about that."

"Man, Charlie was something else. To this day, I've never met a kid like her."

15 years ago

Charlie lay her head against the window frame on the door of the back-seat. The window was down, and the hot summer air was whipping through the top of her hair. Her older brothers were in the front seat talking about girls, and Charlie had tuned them out miles ago. It was just weeks past her 13th birthday, and this was her first unsupervised teen outing with other teens from her school. The two-lane road was curvy and covered with trees overhead. It had been a long summer, and Charlie wasn't looking forward to starting the new school year. Her cousin, Rylan, sitting next to her, was in from up north and stayed with Charlie's family for the summer, but her trip was almost over, and next week she would be returning home. Charlie wasn't sure who's idea it was to hike the woods at Bluffton, but she didn't care. She was just glad to be included.

They had gotten up early that morning and left just as the sun was coming up. She and Rylan both wore denim shorts over their swimsuits, got into the car, and fell asleep again before they'd hit the main road. Awake now, Charlie was enjoying the wind in her hair as she watched the trees zoom by. In the car behind them was James, Roger, Vincent, and Farmer. Farmer was driving. And Aaron and Sam were supposed to meet them there with some of the upperclassmen from the school. Sam didn't have a license yet, but no one would ever know that. Both Sam and Aaron had been driving since they were old enough to see over the steering wheel. Sam had an old Wrangler Jeep he'd been fixing up for as long as anyone could remember, and he planned to load as many people as he could into it and bring it to Bluffton Creek.

Charlie's older brother turned the car into a small gravel road and drove slowly as the gravel dust rose behind them in a cloud. Charlie sat up and shook Rylan, "We're here." She said. Rylan stretched and yawned, "Good cause I have to pee." She said in her perfectly northern way. Charlie's brother stopped and jerked the gear into park, and they began to climb out of the car. Sam and Aaron were already there with two girls and two guys from school. As soon as Sam and Aaron joined Charlie and her carload, the two girls and two guys took off to do their own thing. It was about that time that Farmer pulled up, and the guys started to get out of the car.

Everyone was standing around in an oddly shaped circle. Farmer, James, and Roger were talking about sports and getting ready for basketball. The older boys were talking amongst themselves about which direction would be the best trail. Sam, Charlie, Aaron, and Vincent were catching up about their week when Rylan came from the trees buttoning her pants after using the bathroom. When Rylan joined the group again, the crowd started to walk towards the trail leading up into the trees but away from Rylan's bathroom break area.

The hot air from the sun's heat was almost smothering, but it was more relaxed on the trail. The trees made a shaded path for them. Halfway up the trail, they came across a creek that let them know they were going in the correct direction. They all took their shoes off and headed into the water. The current was steady but not strong due to the lack of rain through the summer months.

The water on their skin felt like bathwater, but the deeper they walked into the creek, the cooler the water was. They all stood in the stream, which was almost knee-deep for Charlie and Rylan, and let the current wash through their legs. Charlie put her fingertips in the water and let the water run through her fingers. The sun shone through the trees and warmed their backs. Charlie's straight long dark hair was in a ponytail, and she felt a slight breeze blow on the back of her neck. Rylan and Sam started flicking water at each other, and their laughter carried through the air and caught the attention of the others standing around.

At the age to notice boys, Charlie began to see what made them attractive to her. Although, she was still too young to understand her feelings or why she felt the way she did. Even so, it was evident to her that Rylan had a crush on Sam, and Sam did not have one on Rylan. But Sam was too friendly to say anything and always treated her kindly. Had Charlie been older and able to understand, she would have realized that Sam didn't have feelings for Rylan but liked having Rylan's attention. It was Sam teasing Rylan, calling her Ryan, that started Rylan's nickname. Every summer, the guys would ask when Ryan was coming, and it always got a laugh from the group.

Although Charlie was honored to have these guys as her friends, she looked at them more like brothers. Maybe as they all got older, she would feel differently but not now. Charlie watched as everyone splashed and flicked water on each other. She laughed at them and joined in the water war. A short time later, they headed to the creek bank to sundry. They put their shoes on, Rylan and Charlie sitting together, and the boys sitting a distance away when Rylan leaned over to Charlie and asked if she was having fun. Rylan was only a few months older than Charlie, but she seemed to be growing up faster than Charlie. Charlie laughed and told her she was.

The boys in a group got up and started heading back onto the trail. As Charlie was finishing the bow on her tennis shoe, Rylan leaned in again and said, "Aaron and Vin keep looking at you."

"Why do I have a booger hangin' out my nose?" Charlie asked, swiping at her nose.

"No, silly," Rylan burst out laughing, "I think one of them likes you."

"Ewe gross!" Charlie exclaimed

Rylan pushed herself from the ground and shrugged her shoulders, "Ok," she said

Charlie sat there for another minute, feeling curiously inside. She smiled to herself, then pushed herself up and ran to catch up with the guys. Again, had Charlie been older, she would have understood that even though she didn't see them as anything other than a brother type, she enjoyed being noticed by the opposite sex.

They had been hiking most of the morning, and the girls were trailing slightly behind the boys. They would stop to look at leaves or flowers. They were in awe of nature surrounding them, especially Rylan. Being from the city, she wasn't used to seeing such beauty. At the same time, the boys focused on getting to the edge of the rocks. Finally, a clearing showed in front of them, and the boys let out a manly cheer. They had made it to the top. The girls looked at each other and laughed as if to say, "Boys." The boys were gathered around the edge of the rock, looking down into the creek below. Charlie and Rylan walked up behind them as they were discussing the depth of the water. Charlie's older brothers and Farmer suggested someone walk down to the creek and check to see how deep it was before they jumped.

They'd been talking about it for more than 5 minutes, and Charlie was getting annoyed. She broke away from the crowd; removed her shoes, slid her pants down over her feet, and folded them; laying them neatly over her shoes. She tilted her head from one side to the other as if to gauge her distance. Without warning, Charlie took off running. As she approached the boys standing around, they parted to let her in. They were confused as to why Charlie was running straight at them. They just stood there as she approached the edge of the rock. Just then, Charlie's oldest brother said, "Charlie Rae NOOO!". But it was too late; Charlie had leaped from the rock's edge and was air born. Just before she hit the water, she stiffened her body like a long slender stick and plummeted into the water; disappearing into the dark blue creek.

Rylan stood with her hand over her mouth. The boys stood with their mouths gaping open, but no one took a breath. Finally, Charlie's two brothers and Sam ran to the rock's edge, and everyone followed behind them. They all stood at the rock's edge, staring into the water for what seemed like an eternity. Then Sam let out a breath and said, "There! I think it see her!" pointing to the area where Charlie went into the water. Bubbles were forming, and water rings started to appear as Charlie emerged. She split the water's surface once again, emerging eyes closed, spewing water and water flowing over her long dark hair. Once her head was entirely above water, she yelled, "woohoo, come on y'all." Everyone standing on the rock's edge breathed finally, and one by one, they began to smile. Sam and Aaron laughed aloud, breaking the tension.

Vin, Aaron, and Sam were the next to kick off their shoes. Vin and Sam made it in next, and Aaron was right behind them. The rest of her classmates followed. It took her brothers and Rylan a couple of extra minutes to regain themselves. Soon everyone was in the creek. They spent the rest of the day jumping into the water, climbing out, and jumping again.

A couple of hours before leaving, the four older hikers joined them at the rock. Everyone was laughing and telling them what Charlie had done. It wasn't the first crazy thing they had seen Charlie do, but it was by far the most outrageous.

Aaron, Vin, and Sam had planned to camp through the weekend at Bluffton Creek. Charlie and Rylan wanted to so badly, but their parents thought they should come home, so that's what they did. However, the following summers, they were able to camp the weekend, and they did every summer until

Charlie's brothers left for college. When Charlie's brother's left for college, they made Farmer promise to watch out for her, which is precisely what he did. He would have done it even if he wasn't asked. Farmer and Charlie had always had a bond. Maybe it's because Farmer was the first to reach out to Charlie and talk to her that day at the playground. Or maybe Farmer just always had a tender place in his heart towards Charlie and felt terrible for her, almost always being the only girl. No one could know why he felt such a sense of responsibility towards Charlie, but Charlie responded to him as an older brother. She trusted him. Their relationship would prove to be one of great value to them both in the years to come.

Present-The Hospital

Aaron pulled into the parking lot of the large white stone building. Despite their efforts to modernize the hospital, the building was old and still looked the same on the outside. The lemon yellow and white laminate tiles still screamed 60's, which is probably the last time the county could afford to update the lobby. Aaron pulled the door to the entry open and headed for the bank of elevators placed directly in front of the entrance. He didn't like small spaces, and elevators were always a challenge for him. However, today Aaron entered the elevator without a thought of his discomfort. He punched the button for the second floor and waited for the doors to close. He wasn't sure exactly where Charlie's room was, but the second floor seemed the best place to start. Unconsciously, he pressed the elevator up button several times before the elevator made its stop at the first-floor lobby.

When the doors opened on the second floor, Aaron went to the nurse's station located just off the elevators and asked for Charlie's room. They directed him to room 207 and told him that her Mother had been here all night and was probably still in the room. Aaron thanked the nurses and headed towards room 207. Aaron, in his hast, had not recognized the nurse or her somber pained face. She had gone to school with Charlie and Aaron, only a few years younger. The nurse hurt for Charlie's Mother and for Aaron and did not envy what he was about to step into. Standing outside the door, Aaron hesitated to go in. He wasn't sure how he would feel seeing Charlie in this position. He had never had to face anything like this before. He turned the knob to the heavy door, and it opened quietly. The knob made a loud reverberation noise as it bounced back into place, and the noise set Aaron on edge again. He slowly entered and looked around the small room for Charlie's Mother, but no one was there except Charlie lying in the hospital bed.

Aaron's eyes fell on Charlie lying there; a fury of emotions welled up in him. Sadness and anger swirled around in his belly. Ultimately, grief took over all the other emotions, and he went to her bedside. Aaron took her hand, careful to avoid the IV. He knelt next to her bed.

"Who did this to you" was the thought that kept repeating in his head.

Charlie's face was bruised, her eyes swollen, she had a cut above her eye and one across her nose. Her upper lip was cracked. She had what appeared to be defensive bruising on her arms. That was just what Aaron could see; he had no idea what damage was under the thick hospital blankets covering her body. He sat with Charlie 20 minutes or so before the door cracked open, and her Mother walked in carrying a cup of coffee.

"Aaron, how are you?" she asked, stunned to find someone in the room.

"I've been better." He said, standing to hug her.

Charlie's Mother proceeded to tell Aaron, Charlie's son Ryan was home when the attack happened. Her son said he saw the man, and the man locked him in his room. Aaron inquired how she was found. Charlie's Mother explained a delivery person came to the house the morning after the attack. Ryan got his attention through his window and asked if his mom was alright. That's when he noticed the front door open. When he investigated the open door and the child alone in the house, he saw Charlie lying on the floor surrounded by blood. When the police arrived, they got Ryan out of his room and got as much information as possible. She had sorrow in her eyes for the child. He was five years old and shouldn't have had to see any of this.

"So, Ryan wasn't hurt at all," Aaron asked.

"No, thank God. He wasn't touched at all." Explained Charlie's Mother.

Aaron and Charlie's Mother took a seat next to Charlie's bed and continued to talk for the next couple of hours. Aaron explained his appreciation to Charlie for her support over the last several years. Her Mother's breath caught in her throat, and she said, "Thank you that means so much to me. She always tends to want to help, especially you boys. She loves you boys."

Aaron bowed his head with a smile on his face, his elbows resting on his knees, "yeah, I think I can speak for all of us when I say the feeling is mutual."

Aaron excused himself from the room and headed towards the lobby on the second floor. There he stood by the bank of windows located across from the elevator. Aaron watched as birds flew over the town of Harriston. Lost in his thoughts of Charlie and their younger years, he didn't hear Vin when he exited the elevator. His best friend, Vin, walked over to Aaron and put his hand on her shoulder. Aaron turned swiftly, shaken from his thoughts.

"Hey Aaron, good to see you." Vin said

Aaron leaned in for a handshake, and a half shoulder hug like men often do. They exchanged hellos, and Aaron explained that he'd seen Charlie and talked to her Mother. Vin asked if Aaron had gotten any other details. Aaron explained that he didn't know anything else except that Ryan had been the hero by getting help.

Vin smiled. "He must take after his mother, strong little boy."

Aaron ran the palm of his hand over his forehead and through his hair "No kidding." He said, shaking his head.

Just then, the elevator doors dinged open with the arrival of the passenger car. When the doors opened, Farmer, Roger, and James exited the elevator. They were all greeting each other. It seemed like a small reunion of sorts. Then an extreme quiet settled over the men as one by one they remembered why they were here. Aaron told them what he knew about the attack, which wasn't much, and he told them about Ryan and how Charlie was found. Although Aaron struggled to keep his anger under control, Farmer and Vin were clearly losing their battle with anger. Vin's handsome fair-skinned face was burning red with suppressed rage at whoever had done this. Farmer's face turned from a nice summer tan to flushed, and his jaw tightened. Roger and James were saddened and heartbroken. Aaron, usually the one known for losing control, had mellowed with age. He'd learned slowly over time how to dismiss the feeling. Although at times he still lost the fight, he mostly could see the anger coming and could take control of the situation. He also learned that attending his AA meetings were a must to stay grounded and in control.

As they stood there in silent reflection, Charlie's Mother walked into the second-floor lobby to see the men standing there together. The image caused her to pause for a moment, and just for a split second, she saw the men as young boys and flashed back to when they were all gathered outside the school, waiting for Charlie to be released from detention. The one and only time Charlie had gotten in trouble at school was defending Farmer and Vin.

13 years ago

Charlie, at age 15, had participated in a work-study through the small private school. She was spending time at the local nursing home assisting the elderly. Charlie had decided the year before that nursing may be the way she wanted to take her future. So, when the school started a program called 'Project Future,' a program the school created with local businesses, Charlie signed up right away. The student could volunteer at their facilities and businesses to earn credits towards school and resumes for colleges. School had been in progress for several months, and Charlie had started at the nursing home at the start of the school year. She volunteered several hours during the week. Charlie was approached by the staff and asked if she could come volunteer for the upcoming weekend. They were having non-medical staffing issues and explained they could use the help. Ultimately, Charlie agrees because she loved her job and she loved helping the residence.

When Saturday morning rolled around, Charlie's brother dropped her off at the nursing facility early on the way to his job. Charlie worked tirelessly with her residents as she always did. When lunch rolled around, she looked forward to sitting in the cafeteria and eating with the residents. Just as she was heading down to the cafeteria, one of the nurses stopped her and ask Charlie to help change some bed sheet. By the time the switch over was complete, lunch with the residents was out of the question. Now she just wanted to get something to eat and finish out her day.

When she got to the cafeteria, everyone had finished lunch and returned to their room. Only the staff remained cleaning up after the lunch rush. She filled her food tray with what was left, creamed corn, and a dried-out beef patty. Much to her surprise, there was banana pudding left, so she grabbed that for dessert. As she was shoveling food into her mouth, she saw some older girls from the public school walk into the cafeteria in a group. Charlie knew the girl's names from around town, but she did not personally know them. She smiled at them with a mouth full of food; they looked at her but didn't respond to her smile.

Unaffected by their response, Charlie kept eating and tried to pay no attention to them. However, they were laughing and talking loudly. Charlie could hear what they were saying without trying to listen. She didn't know who they were talking about but what they were saying was not complimentary to the individual. Then she heard one of the girls say, "Frickin' Otis Farmer thinks he's too good to date me." The girl said with her hand on her heart in mock disbelief.

Charlie stopped midchew of her beef patty. She could feel her neck growing red. She had a cheek full of beef and started to chew again slowly, but her hand was gripped on the fork so tightly it began to hurt her fingers. It was then that Charlie realized she was gripping the fork tightly. She tried to calm the rage by telling herself she would call Farmer when she got home and stop it before these nasty comments got out around town. Just as her neck started to fade back to normal, Charlie heard Vin's name come from one of the girls. The bite of dry meat Charlie was in the middle of swallowing seemed to grow bigger and drier and stuck in her throat on the way down. She took a drink of water to wash the meat down and tried to listen to what they were saying about Vin calmly. But again, the comments spoken about Vin were not complimentary. She was able to keep her calm until the girls began to laugh even more loudly and began to trade insults randomly about both Vin and Farmer.

Charlie took a deep breath and stood to her feet. She straightened out her uniform and picked up her tray of half-eaten food, and began carrying it to the trash, which happened to be located just past the group of girls. As she passed the girls, she looked at them to ensure she knew the girl's names to tell Vin and Farmer who was talking about them. As she looked at the girls, one stopped her and said, "Aren't you one of those private school kids?"

Charlie stopped and said, "Yeah." The tone of her voice neither angry nor sassy. Just a simple 'yes' to politely acknowledge a question.

Another girl said, "So you know Vincent and Farmer?"

Charlie nodded her head slowly and again flatly said, "yup, but you don't." and started to walk away.

Just as Charlie had walked past the girls, she heard one of them laugh and say, "Bitch."

The red color in Charlie's neck rose to her face, and she walked back to the seated girls. Charlie looked down at them and asked, "What did you say?"

The girls were quiet and looked at each other as if they had no idea what she was talking about. Then one of the girls said, "I called you a bitch. All y'all think you are so much better."

Charlie looked her directly in the eyes. She starred in her eyes a little longer than expected, just enough to make the girl uncomfortable. The girl began to wiggle in her seat a little. About that time, Charlie took her bowl of cream corn and dumped it on the girl's hair. The other three girls gasped and just looked; mouths gapped open. Charlie said, "Oh, we are too good for people like you. No doubt about that."

Charlie walked away. She threw the rest of her food in the trash and walked out of the cafeteria as if nothing had happened. Charlie knew she would eventually be in trouble, and she didn't care. At least now, the girls had something tangible to talk about. What Charlie had done spread like wildfire through the halls of both schools. Rather than Vin and Farmer and what they had supposedly done being the topic of conversation, Charlie was the big gossip. Privately her older brothers were proud of Charlie; however, publicly, they shook their heads at her actions.

The following Monday, Charlie was called into the principal's office. She wasn't surprised, and she knew that the nursing facility would have to tell the school what she'd done. As Charlie approached the door to the principal's office, the door was closed. Before she opened the door, she paused outside the closed door collecting herself. She could hear laughter inside. She stood there for a moment, waiting for them to stop laughing when she heard one of the men inside say through laughter, "What are we going to do with Charlie?"

The other man said, "Let's see what she tells us."

Charlie knocked on the door to the principal's office, and she could hear them clearing their throat and shifting in their chairs, apparently trying to compose themselves. She opened the door to her principal and the high school English teacher, who was also the head of the Project Future program. Charlie was asked about the incident. Rather than trying to get out of her punishment, she decided just to tell the truth. To the credit of both the men in the office, they did not show any emotion and handled themselves very professionally. Charlie sat there like a baby bird, her blue eyes wide in anticipation, her brown hair pulled back, wisps were falling out of her ponytail into her face. Both men looked into their laps for a long minute of silence. Finally, the principal spoke. He announced two days detention, and it would not reflect her permanent record if she apologized to the nursing facility.

Charlie thanked them and left the office, closing the door behind her. As soon as the door clicked closed, she could hear muffled laughter again, and the English teacher said through a burst of laughter, "creamed corn." She wasn't exactly sure what was funny, but something had gotten them tickled. She was relieved because that must have put them in a good mood. She felt the punishment was very lite considering the crime, but she would take it.

Charlie's Mother remembered the boys standing outside the school when she pulled up to the door to pick 15 year old Charlie up from detention. They stood there in a huddle, looking at the ground but waiting patiently. When Charlie's Mother approached the boys, she said, "boys," Greeting them as she walked by. The boys all returned an "Evening ma'am" just as Charlie was exiting the building. The boys swarmed to her like flies to honey. They all asked questions and slapped her on the back in a thank you kind of way. Charlie wasn't sure how any of this got out to the school. She didn't know how the guys knew about it either, but they did, and they were 100% supportive, which made her punishment feel even more tolerable.

It wasn't until years later that she talked to the principal and the story came up after she graduated and married. He'd told Charlie that it was so hard for them to keep their composure during that meeting. All the two men could visualize was Charlie throwing cream corn on the girl. At that time, the principal told Charlie, "You had a lot of fire in your belly back then. I didn't know if we'd get you through or not."

Charlie laughed and realized, compared to the adults she knew now, from college and then working, she did have a bit of a wild streak in her, and maybe she still did. However, back then, she didn't think anything of it. She was just doing what felt right. Doing what felt right had served her well back then, which is why she kept following that feeling as an adult

The principal said, "it was then that all of us teachers realized how close the 6 of you were. As you should be. But that's when someone came up with the name 'Charlie and the faithful five'". It was around 8th grade that she remembered hearing the name of their gang of friends. She didn't know how they got it or why. She'd ask her mother why Charlie's faithful five. And her mother said, "Well, it looks like y'all will make it together to graduation. Most kids come and go from the school, but you all have stayed faithful all the way through." At the time, the explanation made sense, and Charlie accepted it as truth. However, as close as they were, not all of them made it to the private school's graduation.

Present-Sam!

Charlie's mother, now standing here watching the faithful five but without Charlie, her eyes whaled up with tears. These boys have stood by their girl, Charlie, for so many years, and Charlie has stood by them. The thought of the connection they must have filled her with emotion.

As she approached the men now, she smiled a loving smile at them and said, "Awe, look here, it's the faithful five all together again."

The men turned around together and, in unison, said, "Hey, there she is." They all walked towards her and took turns giving her hugs.

"Well, boys, I'm going for more coffee, would anyone like one?" Her mother said as she walked towards the elevator. They all responded, "No, Thank you." So, she proceeded on to the elevator and her task at hand.

The guys all decided it was time to take a few minutes with Charlie, so they began to walk towards Charlie's room. The group approached the door, and Aaron slowly entered first. Farmer followed up the group and joined last. Before he entered, he wiped his hands on his jeans, took a deep breath, then walked in. The men gathered around Charlie as she lay in her hospital bed, covered with warm blankets up to her chest. Her arms were uncovered and lying lifeless on top of the blankets.

She had a breathing tube inserted in her mouth, and her mouth was taped closed to hold the tube in place.

That sight alone would have been enough to push Farmer and Vin over the edge, but then there were the bruises and cuts on her face and around her eyes and lips. Her arms and hands were bruised. There was a breathless moment of silence, and not one of them could take a deep breath. Aaron stepped forward to her bedside and gently picked up Charlie's hand. Just then, Vin released a whimper, like a disappointed child, and tears began to stream down his face. He excused himself, saying, "Sorry, I, I'll be back." He walked into the hall.

James' eyes were wide, and his mouth gaped open in pure astonishment, "Who could do this? Why would anyone do this to her."

Roger, head down shaking it vigorously, "It makes no sense."

Outside the room, Charlie's mother returned from getting coffee when she saw Vin standing outside Charlie's door, head in hands, crying. She walked to him and took him in her arms, "I know, sweetheart. It's a lot to take in." she said, holding him, trying to comfort him as a mother does. She noticed Vin was still crying, so she continued, "She always loved you boys, even though she knew there would be a time you all grew apart, she loved you all." She paused then said, "You were her first love, and a girl doesn't forget that, ever."

Vin broke from the embrace and wiped his eyes, "I know, I felt that way for her as well." He wiped his nose with his sleeve and tried to compose himself so that he could return to Charlie's room. Charlie's mother explained she knew it looked terrible. She also explained some other injuries they couldn't see. Fractured and bruised ribs, bruises to her back, kick marks on her lower back and legs. She explained the coma seemed to be caused by a head wound. Vin was devastated and asked if there was anyone her mother could think of that would do this. But she could not imagine anyone wanting to hurt her daughter this way.

After Vin had regained his composure and taken control of his temper, He and Charlie's mother returned to the room. There they found Aaron sitting in a chair next to Charlie's bed, holding her hand. Roger and James were standing at the foot of the bed, and Farmer was standing next to Aaron. Farmer was rubbing his hand over her hair as gently as a father would rub his newborn child's head.

James was the first to break the silence, "We have to find out what happened, who did this."

Roger disagreed, "No, I think we should let the police handle it."

"I know all too well how the police handle this shit," James said, then looked to Charlie's mother, "Sorry, I didn't mean to curse."

She shrugged. "It's ok. Emotions are high. This has all gotten our blood boilin."

James continued, "The police in this town aren't equipped to handle this. They are the same old farts that were around when we were kids. All they do all day is sit up at the Hardee's eating their free ice cream cones and drinking their free coffee."

Aaron and Farmer agreed with James and were nodding their heads as James talked. Aaron wasn't fond of police anyway due to his run-ins and experience with the law in Harriston. James was an attorney and knew all too well how the Harriston police worked. He'd been protesting for years to get new and younger recruits in from the state.

Roger interrupted James, "We got to keep our heads about us. We can't just go off half-cocked. The police will lock us out entirely if they feel threatened."

"Maybe they need to feel a little threatened. Over half of those old men should have retired ten years ago." Farmer said, and Roger did agree with that statement.

Charlie's mother sat in silence, listening to the boys vent their frustrations. She looked at each man as he spoke but never interfered. She assumed their conversation was a display of their anger. She'd felt the same way when she first saw Charlie. Who wouldn't want to find the person who'd done this and hold him responsible for such an act of violence?

Vin finally spoke up, "We shouldn't argue in here. Charlie hated when we disagreed."

Farmer said, "You know what, Vin is right. Let's say goodbye for now and go discuss this in the lobby."

They all agreed, and Charlie's mother asked, "Can someone come back tonight and sit with her. I need to make a trip home."

Aaron stepped up before anyone else could and agreed to stay the night so she could go home and get some rest.

"Thank you, if she wakes up, I want someone to be here." Charlie's mother said, and they all agreed it was for the best.

"We will work it out for you," Vin said, looking at her.

The men had left Charlie's room in a huddle, the same way they had arrived and were seated in the second-floor lobby. They discussed a plan of action as to how best to obtain information and stay off the police radar as long as possible. James had connections at the courthouse and said he'd contact them to find out if they had heard anything. Roger was saying they needed to keep a low profile because the local newspaper would undoubtedly have a story in tomorrow's paper, when behind them, they heard someone say in a gravelly smoker's voice, "Well, look at this bunch of sons of bitches."

The five men turned to see a man standing, hands punched down in his pockets, in faded blue jeans and clean but worn work boots. His misshapen tee-shirt looked as if it had seen many years of washes and wear. The men didn't need to see the man to recognize the voice. They only turned to see if it was Sam. And there he was, standing in front of them.

Aaron was the first to turn his back to Sam, "Dammit, Sam, what are you doing here?" Aaron asked.

"I may not have graduated with you shitheads, but I'm still part of this group. Y'all know I love that girl too." Sam said, "No one thought to call me, hum? Y'all too good to tell me?" Sam finished as he walked towards the group of men sitting down.

Farmer stood up and put his hand out, "Sam, if you came to cause trouble, we don't need any of that right now."

Sam laughed a deep sarcastic laugh, "Ain't none of y'all know me anymore. You don't know the first thing about me." Sam said, shaking his head. He looked to the ground and pursed his lips. "I'm just here to see Charlie and her parents. Then I'll go."

10 Years Earlier

At the end of Sam's junior year, Sam had started trying out a different type of rebellion. He'd always had a rebellious streak to him, but after his father's death, he'd become even more so. Aaron was usually right next to him accept Aaron still cared and mostly stayed away from anything that would get him caught. Sam didn't care, and he would do what he wanted without thought to the consequences. It was at this time that Sam had gotten caught for smoking in the school parking lot. Luckily for Sam, it was only tobacco when he got caught. Any other night he would have been caught with something a lot more potent.

Nonetheless, tobacco was prohibited for all students, and the school board had no choice but to expel Sam. The group was heartbroken. One of their own would not be there for their senior year. Although Sam acted as if he didn't care, Charlie had seen him outside the church one evening. They began to talk. Sam confided in her that he was angry the whole thing happened. Sam told her he didn't know why he kept doing the stupid things he was doing because he knew they were wrong for him and would only get him in deeper trouble. Charlie listened to Sam. She understood his fight with good and evil, right and wrong. She couldn't understand his level, but she understood the internal fight and told him as much.

Although Sam didn't graduate with the group, he did graduate from the public school. Charlie had heard he'd had trouble there too. She tried to reach out to him as much as possible. Sam was always appreciative of her for that. Sam still joined in with the group for events that weren't school-related. It wasn't as if he were gone entirely from their lives. After graduation, Sam got a job at one of the local factories. Charlie and Sam continued to stay in touch. Soon Charlie was off to college, but the summer before college, Charlie started to run into Sam almost everywhere she went. Sam and Charlie spent that summer together. They spent every spare moment they had together. They walked by the creek and swam. They would meet up at the park and lay on the picnic tables watching the stars. Sometimes they would just ride in Sam's old Jeep until they found a field they could lay in. Sometimes they would roam the fields and pick flowers then give them to each other. They spent the summer laughing together and remembering past times. They had serious in-depth conversations about the future and what was expected of them. Charlie felt like if Sam was with her, he was staying out of trouble.

Before Charlie left for college, she and Sam were lying in a field, watching the clouds move over the stars and moon. The summer night air was hot and thick even though the sun had gone down. Charlie was in a tank top and jean shorts. Sam was shirtless and in camouflaged cargo shorts. Both were shoeless and sticky from dried sweat from the humid day.

Sam looked to Charlie, "Your unusually quiet tonight."

Charlie said, "I'm sorry, I have a lot going on in my mind. I'm just trying to sort it all out."

Sam ran a knuckle down her arm, "Hey, you can tell me if you want."

Without taking her eyes off the stars, she said, "I don't want to go to college a virgin. It's embarrassing, and I probably shouldn't tell you that, but that is what's on my mind."

Sam looked away from her to the stars, "You don't have to if you don't want to. I'm not saying it in a creepy way. I'm just saying it's an option."

Charlie laughed, "Oh, you would be willing to sacrifice for me. Is that what you are saying. That's oh so generous of you."

Sam laughed, "I knew you would take it that way." He said and put his hand on Charlie's arm, gently holding her arm. He said, "Look, we made it all summer without the boys finding out about us hanging out all the time. Honestly, I don't know how we pulled it off, but I've enjoyed your company. It's been good for me. If you want, we can, it's totally up to you, and no one will ever have to know you lost it to me."

Charlie turned to her side and propped her head on her hand, "I'd be scared? Would you be gentle? Take it slow?" she asked, almost whispering.

Charlie couldn't believe she was even entertaining this idea. Sure, she had explored the thought of Sam in that way from time to time over the summer. But she knew Sam was not the settling down type, and there was no future with him. Now laying here next to him, the future isn't what this was about.

Sam put his hand on her cheek and rubbed a thumb under her eye to wipe away a bead of sweat, "Charlie, I'd never do anything to hurt you, and I would never do anything you didn't want me to do."

Charlie leaned into Sam, and Sam leaned into Charlie. Sam put his lips so close to Charlie's she could almost feel the electricity coming from Sam's body. Charlie knew this was the very moment of no return. If she leaned in anymore, they would kiss, and if they kissed, she would let Sam take her virginity. Charlie left Sam hanging there just millimeters from her lips. She made him wait for her, and he did. She placed her hand over his hand that still rested on her cheek, and she leaned into Sam, finally letting him kiss her. The kiss was soft and slow. She could feel his dry summer lips on hers. Her body immediately reacted to him. Once their lips touched, something strange connected within her. Charlie felt as if a place deep inside her was being filled. A place she hadn't known was empty. She let Sam kiss her deeply, and the more intense the kisses became, the more Charlie felt comfort and peace fill that unknown empty spot.

Sam's lips left hers and trailed down her neck. Charlie laid flat on her back while he continued to kiss her. Sam began to run a hand along Charlie's side and over her tank top to her breast. Charlie's reaction to his touch immediately made Sam grow hard, and as he moved closer to Charlie, she could feel him hard against her. They had only begun to kiss, and already Charlie was aching for Sam, but Sam told her, "I want to take it slow. I want you to feel this entire experience." Sam wanted to go slow and let Charlie feel everything this intimate experience had to offer. He wanted her encounter with intimacy to be whole. Over the years, Sam had heard many girl's stories of disappointed firsts. He did not want that for Charlie.

Charlie nodded that she understood, and Sam began to unbutton her shorts while still kissing her neck. His breath warm on her, even warmer than the summer night air. Charlie put her hands on Sam's muscular chest and ran them along his sides and to his back. She could feel his muscles moving under his skin every time he would shift positions. They were so close to one another now, and Sam could feel Charlie breathing deep breaths against his chest.

Sam continued to take things slow for Charlie. By the time Charlie climaxed, Sam had touched and kissed every part of her body. Sam repeatedly asked if he was hurting her or if she liked what he was doing. The more Charlie spoke to him or affirmed his touches; Sam enjoyed himself. His eyes never left hers as they completed.

Sam smiled at Charlie's moon lit face and the moonlight glistening off her breasts. Her legs were shaking, and her breath was ragged and shallow. Sam knew the sight of Charlie he saw right now would be forever tattooed in his memory; soft pale moon lit skin, sweat beads glistening, her perfect half-smile, her huge brown curious eyes looking deeply into him, and her long dark hair spread amidst the blanket. Sam had often wondered what it would be like to be with Charlie. However, as satisfied as he was this experience, it did little to resolve his desire to be with her. Sam wanted to take her away from this world and protect her. He wanted to ensure that no one would ever hurt her.

Charlie, cheerful, pleased with the outcome, giggled and scooted her back into Sam's chest. As they laid in the spoon position, Sam took the edges of the blanket and wrapped it over them. Charlie fell asleep resting her head on Sam's arm like a pillow, and Sam curled into Charlie.

When they woke the following day, the sun was already up and shining down on them. They dressed, jumped in Sam's Jeep, and headed to the main road. As they headed home, Charlie leaned her head back and let the wind blow through her hair. Her hand was out the Jeep door, and she was letting it ride the wave of the wind. Sam pulled into Charlie's driveway and let her out.

"Will you be there tonight?" She asked Sam

"Maybe," he replied

"Then maybe I will see you tonight." She said as she quietly shut the Jeep door.

He watched Charlie walk to her house. He thought to himself, "that right there is a beautiful woman." Charlie pulled open her bedroom window and crawled in. Before she shut it, she waved to Sam, and he took off down the road."

That night was the big Junior/Senior field party. Everyone came to welcome the new seniors and send off the new college students. As she climbed into her bed, she reminded herself to thank Sam for this summer if she saw him at the field party. This was the first summer in many years. Rylan hadn't come to visit for the summer. Sam had helped her get through it without her. Rylan had become somewhat of a mystery to Charlie. She obviously grew up faster than Charlie, but it seemed as if she had started everything and tried everything years before Charlie. She drank, smoked, tried marijuana, and even had sex years before Charlie. It was all new and exciting to Charlie, but these things were just another day in Rylan's life. Sam had truly been a godsend to Charlie this summer in more ways than he would ever realize. She rode the memory of Sam all way to deep REM sleep with a slight smile on her lips.

That night she pulled into the Webster's field and parked her old hand-me-down truck behind everyone else's old hand-me-down trucks and SUVs. The sun was just setting, so Charlie checked her lips and slid her lip gloss in her back pocket. She hoped that Lockhart wouldn't be there, although he was a senior this year, so chances were, he would be there. If for nothing else, just to taunt her.

Lockhart or Lock was a comer or goer to the school. No one expected him to last as long as he had. When he arrived, they all tried to include him, but he just didn't fit. The school was mostly void of cliques, but Lock made his own clique. Lock didn't want to be at the school, and he was angry at everyone. He taunted Charlie at school every day even though he was a year younger than her. Sam hated him. Even if he wasn't there every day, he hated Lock. None of the guys had much respect for him for the way he spoke to Charlie or the way he treated other people.

As Charlie approached the crowd, she saw a couple of girls standing on the edge of the field. They were becoming seniors this year, so they were just a year younger than Charlie. Charlie waved to them, and they all hugged her. They greeted one another and started to head to the bonfire. Just as they stepped forward, Lock ran in front of them and stopped them. Two of the girls rolled their eyes to him as he said, "Charlie, your ass looks fine tonight. I could bend you over and…." One of the girls pushed him as she yelled, "Lock, shut up." The girls split and walked around him, meeting back together once they had passed him. They proceeded to talk about their summer and asked about each other's summers. The girls had left to find beer, and Charlie stood alone by the fire when Farmer, Vin, and Aaron walked up.

They were standing around the fire talking when Lock wondered up, "Hey guys, so which one of you is taking Charlie home tonight?" he said as he gulped the last of his beer, crushed the can in his hand, and carelessly tossed it to the ground.

Aaron stepped to him with his hands bunched in fists. Farmer put his hand on Aaron's shoulder, and Aaron stopped, "Let him say one more thing to us. Damn, I hate that guy. Let him give me a reason." Aaron said, unclenching and clenching his fists.

Vin said, "I know I've been patient all year, one wrong word."

They all agreed it wouldn't take much for any of them to have a reason to fight Lock. As they discussed what they would like to do to Lock, Sam walked up to the group carrying beers by the plastic ring holding them all together. "What's up guys?" Sam asked, ripping a beer from its plastic ring and handing it to Charlie. As the guys answered Sam, he was giving each of them a beer. Sam was looking past them, looking for Lock, "I hate that guy, asshole." They all snapped their beers open and sipped the foam as it fizzed through the opening. Charlie said, "To our awesome summer." They all agreed and raised their cans in the air, then they all united took a sip. Sam took a gulp and smacked his lips as he lowered the can.

They talked a few more minutes, and then Sam announced he had to go to the Jeep for more beer. Charlie said, "Hey, I have to pee. Can I come with you?" Sam shrugged and waved his hand at Charlie, "Com'on." On the way to the Jeep, Charlie talked to Sam about how much she appreciated his company this summer. When they got to the Jeep, Sam handed her a flashlight, and she headed to the woods to use the bathroom. Sam called after her, "Want me to wait?"

"No, I'll find you all in a minute," Charlie called back and then disappeared in the tree line.

With arms full of beers, Sam headed towards the fire to meet back up with the guys.

Charlie had finished her business and was working her way out of the trees to the open field. She shined her light beam up to find Lock standing there waiting for her. "What the hell, Lock, you scared me," Charlie said

"Oh, am I that scary?" he said with a cigarette hanging out of his mouth.

"No, I'm not scared of you." She said, trying to move past him.

"You should be." He said, eyeing her up and down. Charlie exhaled and dropped her shoulders. She pushed him to move him out of her way. She muttered "Asshole" under her breath. Lock grabbed her upper arm hard, but Charlie didn't make a noise. She just looked him in the eyes with a discusted look on her face. Charlie could feel the rage in her belly whaling up. She yelled loudly, "Get the fuck off me!" and swung wildly. Her fist made contact with Lock's face, and he grabbed his nose. About then, Sam came from the dark and pushed Lock to the ground. He stood over top of him about to land punches of his own when Farmer and Aaron came and pulled Sam back. Aaron was the last to arrive and put himself between Lock, who was still on the ground, and Sam.

Lock stood up and was muttering, "Fuckin' bitch bloodied my nose." Aaron turned and looked at Lock. You better leave before I kick your ass myself." Aaron said through clenched teeth. The guys checked Charlie, and she assured them she was okay. Lock left the party that night, and Charlie didn't see him again until the following summer.

A few days after the party, Charlie left for college. She called and wrote to the guys to keep in contact. She knew if she didn't, they wouldn't because they are guys and don't think that way. As time went on, she heard less and less from Sam. She was hearing from the guys that he worked a lot and was drinking a lot, but he was alright.

The truth was that Sam was carrying on an affair with a co-worker at the factory. What the guys didn't know, she was supposed to be getting divorced and staying with Sam. However, when she discovered she was pregnant, she went back to her husband, leaving Sam in utter confusion. He didn't know if the child was his, and he didn't know what his future with her would hold. Many times, he considered calling Charlie for advice but thought better of it. Sam soon realized he'd never loved the woman. He'd only loved the idea of having a woman and a baby in his life.

After many one-night stands and many drunken nights stumbling home, he found out one of his one-night stands had a baby and claimed it was his. After paternity testing and court battles, he found out the child was his, and in Sam's good-hearted fashion, he took his responsibility like the man he was. He even tried to make it work with the child's mother, but that was short-lived.

For years Sam just worked and lived his life. His child was older now, and he was enjoying his child's older years. They had a little more freedom to go places together and play basketball at the park and fish together. Sam and his son were out at a breakfast buffet in town when he overheard a deputy talking about a woman's attack on the old route. His ears pricked up. His mother lived out that way. He immediately flipped his cell phone open and called his mother. She answered on the first ring. She was surprised to hear from him. She hadn't heard from him in over a year. He asked her about the attack, and she told him it was Charlie. She told him his brother and the boys were headed over to the hospital. When he hung up, he called his son's mother and arranged to have her pick him up early so he could go to the hospital as well. On the way to the hospital, he'd stopped in a field and picked Charlie some flowers, like they use to do, years ago. But before he entered the hospital, he'd thrown them in the trash. The last time Sam had seen Charlie was a couple of years after her college graduation. He knew he'd messed up the last he'd seen Charlie, and there was no amount of flowers that would fix that.

Present-Sam Sees Charlie

Sam was walking down the empty hall to Charlie's hospital room. Images of her tanned, sun-soaked face flashed to memory. He remembered seeing her in the moonlight the night he'd taken her virginity. He remembered her in her soaking wet swimsuit climbing from the water at Bluffton's creek. He remembered her throwing her head back in his Jeep and laughing, mouth wide open and eyes sparkling. He remembered looking at her in his Jeep, bare feet on the dash as she sang every word to Pat Benatar's Bad Reputation as it played on the radio. She would look over at him and sing the words to him.

He opened the door, and when he entered, the hospital room was empty of visitors. He closed the door behind him. He slowly walked to Charlie's bedside.

His eyes at the sight of Charlie immediately filled, and a whimper escaped his lips. His mind flashed to Charlie the first time he'd met her. She'd just fallen from the tree after trying to catch a snake. He'd looked down at her, sucking in the air that had been knocked out of her. Her bright blue eyes wide, and the corners of her mouth curled about to smile. Her dark hair was spread out all over the ground and blowing in her face.

The memory of her and the image of her now was more than he could carry. He broke down and fell to his knees next to her bed. He took her weak hand in both of his and brought it to his lips. His tears were falling on her hand, but he didn't notice. So many emotions were pulsing through him, but anger was slowly winning. The more he tried to hold his tears back, the more tears came. He cried so forcefully his shoulders were shaking as he cried into his hands. Finally, his tears stopped; still wracked with a pain in his heart, he quickly left the room and walked directly to the elevator. He didn't stop to talk to the group of friends sitting in the lobby. He headed straight to his truck, turned the key in the ignition, and drove away. He drove with no destination in mind. He aimlessly drove back roads. Occasionally he would stop and pick several flowers, which he set in the passenger seat next to him, but then would get back in his truck and continue to drive.

Eventually, he found himself parked in the parking lot of the only bar in Harriston. Sure, other restaurants served food and alcohol, but this only served alcohol. And good church-going Harristonites didn't go here. Sam sat in the parking lot for a long time, contemplating if he should go in or not.

Present-Hospital

The men saw Sam enter the elevator. Obviously upset, Aaron stood to go after him. Farmer stopped him. "Let him go. He needs time." Farmer told Aaron. Aaron sat back down. Moments later, Aaron and Vin went to sit with Charlie again. Roger and James headed to James' office at the courthouse. Farmer left to go back to his house. However, Farmer didn't return home. He was driving home when he decided to go to Charlie's house. He pulled into her long driveway and parked in front of the house. He walked up the porch stairs, and they cricked under his weight. He stood at the front door and looked around. Nothing looked out of place at first sight. He looked closely at the door, and he could see where the jam of the doorway had been splintered. He wondered why there wasn't police tape on the door. He looked in the windows and saw where Charlie had been lying when she was found. Trying to divert his eye from the sight of her blood, he looked around the room.

He saw her couch, where she usually sat to read. He saw a blanket spread on the couch like she had been using it. And he saw the table that sits next to the couch, and the drawer was slightly open. Farmer walked around the back of the cabin and let himself in by opening a window and crawling through. The house, except for the blood-stained carpet, was in order. Nothing seemed out of place. He looked down at the slightly ajar drawer and saw a cell phone. "What the hell." Farmer said aloud to the empty room. He picked up the cell phone and pushed the power button, but the phone was dead. Farmer let himself out the way he had come in and lowered the window back to the closed position. He drove to the nearest gas station and bought a phone charger to fit Charlie's phone.

Once home Farmer plugged up the charger and inserted the cord into the phone. He called James, who was still with Roger, and told him what he'd found. James told Farmer to let him know what he finds when the phone charges up, and they disconnected the call. Farmer tried to stay busy while the cell phone charged. Eventually, he decides to ride his tractor for a while. He took the tractor down to his back field and started to mow. Mowing was Farmer's happy place. During the years of his failing marriage, he'd spent more time on the tractor than in the house.

That night Aaron and Vin were riding around in Aaron's SUV when they passed the bar of Harriston. They saw Sam's truck in the parking lot and decided they should check in on Sam. When they entered the bar, they saw Sam sitting on a stool at the bar. Sam was turning a tumbler full of whiskey between his thumb and forefinger. Vin took a seat at a table on the bar room floor and let Aaron approach Sam on his own. Aaron took a seat at the bar next to Sam, and ordered soda water from the bartender. Sam looked at Aaron then back at his whiskey. Sam looked dissolved, his eyes were red and swollen. He looked like he'd been drinking, but he was sober. Sam asked Aaron why he was in the bar.

"I came to check on you." Aaron said, "You're still my brother." Aaron took a sip of his soda water.

Sam said, "You shouldn't be here, neither should I for that matter."

Aaron looked curiously at Sam but didn't question him. Sam stared hard at the whiskey in his hand and told Aaron, "I've been sober for over a year. This is the first time I've seriously considered breaking my sobriety."

Aaron wiped a hand over his face, "Man, I didn't know. I thought you'd been on a bender." Sam puffed out a laugh, "I know. I figured if you didn't know and I screwed this up, I wouldn't let anyone down. Again."

Aaron turned to Sam, "Man, you don't have to do this alone. I've been there we can support each other. I'll admit, if there was something to cause me to drink, this is it. But man, you don't have to do this; the decision is still yours."

Sam scooted his tumbler of whiskey towards the bartender, turned to Aaron, and said, "Will you take me home." Sam said more as a statement than a question. Aaron nodded and stood up from his barstool, nodded to Vin to head towards the door, and the three men exited the bar. They rode silently to Sam's house. Aaron turned the engine off when they pulled into the driveway, but they just sat in the SUV. Finally, Sam said, "You all are welcome to stay here tonight." Without a word, the three men exited the SUV and loaded into Sam's small house. Sam lay on his bed fully clothed and fell asleep almost immediately. Aaron and Vin took their place on Sam's sectional sofa, and both fell asleep.

The following day Aaron woke up and made his way to Sam's kitchen to make coffee, but he found the coffee pot was full of fresh coffee. He looked to the couch, but Vin was still asleep. He found Sam on his back deck. Aaron filled a cup with coffee and went to see Sam. Sam was shirtless, beating the hell out of a punching bag hanging from the back deck's exposed beam. Sam had earbuds in and didn't hear Aaron come to the deck. Aaron just stood there watching Sam take his anger out on the bag. Sam saw Aaron from the corner of his eye and stopped his activity. Both Sam and Aaron sat at a small table on the back deck. Sam wiped his face with a rag and rested his face in his hands. "Aaron, I love her. I guess I've always loved her." Sam said with his face still in his hands.

Aaron nodded, "I know, we all do. She's been a staple for all of us in life. At some point, we have all needed her."

Sam raised his head from his hands and stared hard into Aaron's eye, "No, man, you don't understand; I love her." Sam said, emphasizing the 'love.' "I've been in love with her for as long as I can remember. I didn't tell you guys because y'all would just think I was drunk or high or whatever. We are supposed to see her as a sister or some shit. But I've never seen her that way. It took me years to realize I loved her, but I think I fell in love with her the first time I saw her." Sam explained.

Aaron, taken by surprise, he'd never have known his brother had kept this secret from him. He was speechless.

Sam continued, "You don't know this, but shortly after Rylan, Charlie's cousin, was killed, you were off to rehab, Farmer was going through his divorce, and Vin was gone doing his artsy shit, and Charlie called me."

Aaron looked at Sam, "She called you, for what?"

Sam continued, "She called me to come get her. She'd gone down to Florida to see what she could find out about Rylan's death. Rylan's mom kept telling her to leave it alone, but Charlie couldn't."

"Did she find anything out? What was she thinking?" Aaron asked somewhat to himself but loud enough for Sam to hear.

Sam shook his head, "I don't know. I don't think she was in her right mind at the time. She was grieving pretty hard and was in complete disbelief. Anyway, she called and asked me to come to get her from Florida. I didn't ask questions; I just drove down and got her."

Aaron sat listening in complete disbelief that neither Charlie nor Sam had let this information out.

"We took a couple of weeks and took our time coming back. Charlie had just lost her husband and then Rylan's death. She needed time to sort things out, and I tried to give it to her."

Aaron's brain started clicking, and the wheels in his head started turning, "Wait a second, shortly after Rylan's death, Charlie moved back to town, and that's when she found out she was pregnant. We all assumed she had gotten pregnant before her husband died." Aaron's mind flashed back to when he first saw Charlie with her baby belly. "You know who else lives in Florida, in the same town Rylan lived in?" Aaron said.

Aaron and Sam both looked up at each other and said in unison, "Lock."

They both jumped from their chairs and pushed their way into the back door of the house. Sam yelled, "Shit!" as he walked into the living room to power up his computer. "If I hadn't been so screwed up back then, I would have put the two together," Sam said, trying to lit a cigarette.

Aaron looked down at Sam, "Well, you thought of it now."

Sam punched the keys on the keyboard and entered Brent Lockhart into the search engine. Sam continued to flick his lighter to get a flame as the computer started clicking internally and finally started to pop results on the screen. Aaron took the lighter and cigarette and lit it for Sam, then handed it back to him. Aaron didn't smoke but used to.

Vin, still on the couch, woke up and sleepily asked, "What's going on" Aaron explained in short detail about Lock living in Florida when Rylan was found dead. Vin said, "Oh yeah, I remember, they thought her death was suspicious, right. I mean, what are the chances Rylan moved from up north down to Florida and moves to the same town as Lock."

Aaron said, "Yeah, but nothing came of it that I remember."

Vin followed up with, "So you think maybe Charlie knew something? But she would tell the police if she knew something."

Sam said, "Yes, unless she got scared and couldn't. Something was definitely going on with Charlie when I picked her up. I just didn't ask."

The computer brought up arrest records for Lock, and according to the records, he was not in jail around the time of Rylan's death nor was he in jail when Charlie would have been down in Florida.

"That doesn't prove anything," Vin said

"No, it doesn't accept that Lock was around and would have had the opportunity to do it," Aaron said. "I have to get back to the hospital. I told Charlie's mother I would stay there this afternoon so she could take care of Charlie's son." Aaron said as he walked to the bathroom to shower.

Sam said, "I'll keep reading. Maybe something will jump out. And Hey, there are clothes in the closet if you want some clean ones."

Vin said he'd stay with Sam and see what they could come up with, "I'll call

Farmer if anything comes of this." Vin said, looking at Sam. Sam agreed with Vin, but Sam's attention never left the screen.

While Aaron was in the shower, he yelled out to Vin and Sam. "See if you can find a phone number or an address for Lock."

Sam said, "OK, I'm on it."

Stacy

The morning after seeing Charlie in the hospital bed, Farmer woke to the sun in his eyes. He'd slept longer than expected. He heaved himself out of bed and headed to the kitchen where Charlie's old cell phone was charging. He thought that the phone was older than Sam's flip phone. He couldn't imagine how Charlie was still using the ancient thing. It had taken all night to charge so that he could get the thing to turn on. He clicked the power button, hoping the phone would power on and keep a charge. The phone lit to life and began to play the official song for the cell carrier the phone was linked to. It didn't take long for Farmer to realize that there was no recent activity on the phone. There were no incoming texts or calls. He clicked the gallery button to see what she had stored in there. And photos popped up of the gang at different outings and events. The picture brought a smile to his face. He came across a picture of Charlie, her bright eyes glowing in the light of the camera flash and her dark hair blowing across her dark, sun-kissed face. She was standing next to her college roommate, Stacy. He looked hard at the picture, focusing on the background, figuring out where the photo was taken, and then realized it was taken at the field party the year after her freshman year of college.

Charlie met Stacy the day she arrived at college, and they had been roommates the four years she stayed there. As far as Farmer knew, Stacy and Charlie were still very close friends. The picture took Farmer back to when Stacy had met the group of guys Charlie called her gang. Stacy seemed to fit right in. She had already heard about all of them and felt like she knew them. That summer, Stacy went everywhere they went. They went to Bluffton creek and jumped the rocks, they went hiking, and to field parties, they went fishing and had fish fry's out in the field. They had camped and went swimming. Stacy did it all and loved it, or so it appeared. Stacy even took an interest in Aaron, and Aaron seemed to have an interest in her. Although Aaron was starting his downward spiral towards alcoholism at the time, no one was aware of it at the time.

The night of the junior-senior field party and Charlie and Stacy were planning to go to the field and then back to college the following morning. Charlie had explained to Stacy this was the summer's main event and would be her last Junior/Senior field party because she had to welcome in the seniors and send off the graduates. They didn't know why but after that, students just didn't go back. It was like their rite of passage had come and gone. Stacy was excited to go. She wanted to see everything and was excited to see Aaron before heading back to college for another year. When Charlie and Stacy arrived, the guys were standing in a group with a beer in their hands and laughing about some joke Vin had made. Sam and Farmer were on call for sober drivers, but they were a year too old to attend so that they wouldn't be amidst the group.

Charlie and Stacy had been there about 20 minutes when Stacy elbowed Charlie to get her attention. Bon Jovi was playing over the speakers loudly about being shot through the heart. Stacy leaned into Charlie and asked, "Who is that creepy guy that keeps staring at you?" Charlie followed Stacy's line of vision and her sights fell on who Stacy was talking about.

Charlie said, "Ewe, don't look him in the eyes. That's Lock. He's the spawn of satan."

Stacy quickly looked away from Lock and looked at Charlie. Charlie remembering that Stacy had not actually seen him before, only his handy work. "Oh yeah, that's him, the evil-doer himself," Charlie said.

Stacy rarely heard Charlie speak negatively about anyone, but she had to agree with Charlie from her limited experience with Lock. Charlie took a sip of her beer and held her empty hand out to Aaron to pass the joint, saying, "Lock is here."

Aaron passed the joint to Charlie. Then Charlie passed it to Stacy. Charlie was in mid-inhale when Def Leppard came over the speakers and started singing about pouring sugar on him. Charlie screamed and coughed and then jumped up and down. She said to Stacy, "Dance with me!" and the girls left to go dance.

Even though Farmer and Sam weren't supposed to be there, they had come together knowing that Lock would be there. They just wanted to make sure Lock minded his own business and didn't get into Charlie's. They sat in Sam's Jeep and watched as the girls danced together. The girl's faces lit by the firelight, and the fire outlined their bodies, making a shadow for Farmer and Sam to keep track of them. They spotted Lock, standing off to himself and a reasonable distance from Charlie and Stacy. They felt comfortable for the moment, and they each cracked open a drink. Beer for Sam and Soda for Farmer. Both Stacy and Charlie had finished their second beer when they started walking away from the group and heading to the line of trees. Sam said, "Pee break." And Farmer nodded in agreement.

About 10 minutes later, Charlie emerged frantically and yelling, "Stacy! Stacy!" Charlie looked to the left and the right. Farmer and Sam both sat upright, spilling their drinks

. They rummaged through Sam's jeep, looking for their flashlights. Charlie ran towards the bonfire. Sam and Farmer weren't far behind her. As the men approached, Sam was looking for Lock. He should have been easy to spot. Standing alone and staring down the visitors as they walked past him. Sam couldn't lay eyes on him. Farmer reached Charlie as she was frantically explaining she couldn't find Stacy. She said they had separated to use the bathroom, and they were talking, then Stacy got quiet. Charlie said she thought Stacy was just using the bathroom, but then she wasn't coming back.

The men took off towards the trees where Charlie and Stacy had entered and shined their flashlights into the wooded area. They were all calling for Stacy, but Stacy was not answering. Farmer said, "She may have slipped and hit her head, or something take me to where you two split up." Charlie led the way.

Stacy hadn't slipped. She was pinned against a tree as Lock had her hands held together in front of her. With one hand, he reached down and lifted her short dress, using his other hand to hold her hands together firmly. Lock licked her neck, and Stacy was whimpered, "Please, don't do this." Stacy could hear Charlie and her friends calling her name, but Lock had told her if she yelled, he'd shoot her right between the eyes. Stacy didn't know Lock well enough to know if he would really do it or not, so she stayed quiet. What little she did know of him she didn't like. Lock had turned Stacy around, so her belly was bend over a tree. He was holding her arms behind her. Stacy was crying and begging him, but Lock hissed against the back of Stacy's neck, "You're even better lookin' than Charlie. This is perfect." He unbuttoned his pants, and they fell to the ground around his ankles. Just as Lock was about to penetrate Stacy from behind, a beam of light fell on Stacy's face, and she felt a firm sideways thrust and then freedom from Lock. She turned around to see Sam and Aaron on top of Lock, holding him to the ground.

Farmer ran to their side, and Stacy ran to find Charlie close by. Sam and Farmer pulled Lock up by his shirt. Charlie ran to Aaron's side. She put her hand on Aaron's shoulder. It took everything within him to hold back his rage. Charlie and Aaron both turned to Stacy, but she assured them she was alright. "Put your fuckin' pants on, asshole," Aaron said as Sam and Farmer dragged Lock over to Stacy. Farmer said, "Here's how we handle these things out here Stacy, we can call the police and file charges, or we can handle it here and now." Stacy, not sure what to say, looked to Charlie. Charlie, holding Stacy as she shook uncontrollably, said, "Stacy, it's up to you. You decide. The guys will honor whatever decision you want, no matter what it is." Stacy straightened up, adjusted her dress, and wiped her face with the back of her hand. Stacy took Charlie's hand and began to walk away. Without looking back, she said, "Do what you want with him, guys." At that point, Lock knew he was in for a world of hurt.

Stacy visited a few more times with Charlie, but she never stayed long or for the whole summer. She would come to see the guys, visit with Charlie's parents and then go home to her family. Stacy and Charlie never spoke of the incident again, and Stacy didn't hold Charlie responsible for it. All she asked is that she and Charlie visit other places instead of going to Charlie's hometown. Charlie, of course, agreed.

The guys had heard from Charlie that after college Stacy had married.

However, the marriage hadn't lasted long, only two years. Stacy was very involved in her career, and that didn't seem to mesh well with her husband at the time, who wanted her home, in the kitchen, probably barefoot and pregnant. Even though Stacy had made it clear that her career would come first for a while after the marriage, her husband wasn't willing to wait. This caused arguments that worsened over time, and eventually, Stacy wasn't willing to fight about it anymore.

Farmer powered off the phone and slid it in his pocket. He decided he would take it by Charlie's mother and Father's house for her to hold on to. Farmer got dressed and headed to Charlie's mother's house. Charlie's parents welcomed him in, as they always did. He didn't waste any time. As soon as he got in the house, he handed them the phone, "I went by Charlie's place last night, and I found her phone." They both looked at him, confused. He noticed their looks but continued, "I thought you might want to keep it for when she wakes up."

Charlie's parents looked at each other and then back to Farmer. Her mother said I guess I don't understand. The police gave us her belongings she came in the hospital with, and I thought her phone was included in that stuff." Charlie's dad was nodding in agreement. He said, "Yeah, we just locked the bag of stuff in the closet in the hospital room with Charlie Rae."

Farmer looked at them, "Really, well, that makes sense. I looked at that phone, and there wasn't anything on there, except a few pictures and some games."

About that time, Ryan, Charlie's son, walked around the corner into the kitchen. Charlie's mother hugged him and said, "You hungry sweet boy?"

Ryan looked at her and said no, but then he looked at her hands and saw the phone, "OH, you found my phone." He grabbed it, put it to his ear, said hello like he was talking to someone, and then walked out of the room.

Farmer smiled, "Well, I guess that clears that up."

As Farmer was leaving, Charlie's mother leaned her head out the screen door and yelled to Farmer, "Stacy is coming to the hospital today. I'm going to try to get there to see her."

Farmer waved to her and got into his car to head to the hospital. When he walked into Charlie's room, Aaron was sitting there with Charlie. They greeted each other, and Farmer filled Aaron in on what he'd been doing. Aaron told Farmer about what they had discovered about Lock and the internet search. Farmer said Charlie's mother said her phone should be here. So did the police even take the time to look at it?"

Aaron said he didn't know, but he hadn't seen the phone. Farmer went to the locked closet and tried to open it. Farmer said, "Her mother said it would be in here. But it's locked."

Aaron walked to the closet, took his pocket knife out, and flipped the blade open. He inserted the knife into the keyhole and twisted. The lock clinked down, and the closet popped open. Aaron said, "They aren't really secure."

Farmer reached into the closet and pulled out the clear plastic bag holding Charlie's belongings. He turned it over in his hands, and the cell phone emerged through the other items in the bag. "There it is!" Farmer said.

He opened the bag and pulled the phone out. He powered it on. It lit up right away. Charlie and Stacy's background picture was the same picture that Farmer had seen earlier on the old phone. Farmer said, Hum, that's weird. I mean, of all the things she could have as her screen saver, she has Stacy on there." When Farmer tried to slide the phone open, there was a lock on it that required a 4-digit code to get into the phone.

He tried a few dates and codes that he could think of, then handed the phone to Aaron, "I can't begin to guess what the code would be."

Aaron took the phone and looked at the picture on the phone, "That's a good picture of them, right?" he kept looking at the picture. Then Farmer noticed Aaron pull the phone closer to his face. Aaron's face scowled, and he was focusing hard.

Aaron said, "You know what's weirder than this picture being on the phone, is that this picture includes Lock."

Farmer Said, "What!?" and grabbed the phone from Aaron. Farmer spread the picture to focus on the areas in the back, and there it was. Lock clearly in the background of the picture.

Aaron said, "You would think she would have cropped him out of the picture."

Farmer agreed that it was strange. The men also decided they could never fully understand Charlie or what she did or didn't do. They both smiled about it and sat in silence for a while, trying to unlock Charlie's phone. They felt, now more than ever, they needed to get that phone open.
When Roger and James showed up, they informed everyone they had not had any luck at the courthouse. Aaron had told them what Farmer had done, Farmer handed the phone over, and Roger and James tried a couple of numbers but had no luck.

Sam And Vin

Sam and Vin left the house. Sam had a handful of printouts. The guys headed towards the hospital in Sam's old Jeep since he had left his truck at the bar. When they arrived at Charlie's room, Sam handed the printouts to Aaron. Sam said the only interesting thing they had found was Lock's phone number and address, and Lock did still live in Florida in the same city Rylan was living in. Aaron asked, "But did he live there at the time of Rylan's death?" Sam answered, "Yes."
Sam said, "I'm going to call Lock and check in on him."

Farmer said, "Ok, that's a good idea. We need to figure out how we can get Charlie's phone open."

The men were discussing plans when Charlie's hospital room door slowly started to open. A pretty, short-haired blond stuck her head in the door. The men all stopped in mid-conversation and turned to look at the lady at the door.

Aaron was the first to break the silence, "Stacy?" Aaron said and started to walk towards the door.

Farmer spoke up, "Oh yeah, Stacy is coming."

At the same time, the guys said, "Ahhh, makes sense," and welcomed Stacy into the room.

"Y'all are all here. That's what makes sense. I should have figured that." Stacy said, giving them each a hug.

They were all catching up with Stacy when she finally asked about Charlie and the circumstances around Charlie's attack.

The guys all got quiet, and Aaron finally spoke up, "Stacy, let's take a walk."

Farmer, in response to Aaron said, "No. No, we will go. We have those things to do we were talking about earlier."

So, the men all headed for the door, saying their goodbyes to Stacy. Aaron proceeded to tell Stacy the details they knew, carefully leaving out the information they discovered during their amateur investigation.

Sam separated himself from the group and dug the phone number and address out of his pocket he'd scribbled down for Lock and dialed the phone number. The phone rang twice and was picked up on the second ring.

Sam said, "Lock, is that you?"

"Yeah, who's this?" Lock asked.

Sam explained who he was, and the phone line was totally quiet, so Sam continued, "anyway, I was wondering if you had a second to talk."

"Um, so let me get this straight," Lock said in his typical sarcastic tone, "You haven't talked to me, in years, the guy that beat the living shit out of me. You called to asked me questions, not to apologize, but to ask me a favor."

Just then, Sam heard a female voice, a voice that Sam recognized. Sam asked, "Is that your mother I hear in the background?"

"Yeah. What of it." Lock said.

"Are you in Harriston? Are you back home?"

"Again, not that it's your business, but yeah. I got in last week. Taking some time with the family. Why do you care?" Lock said.

Sam was reeling, Lock is here in town, and was here when Charlie was attacked. His brain was racing. He had an instant change of plan. "Lock, meet me at the Harriston bar tonight at 8."

Lock laughed sarcastically again, "And why would I do that?"

Sam said, "Let's just say if you don't, your parents will never want to claim you again, and you will have to deal with a couple of my friends and me again."

Lock grunted and said, "Fine." Then disconnected the phone line.

Sam clicked the flip phone closed and slipped it in his pocket. He walked as fast as he could back to the guys who were mulling around their cars which were parked in the parking lot in a row. Sam approached them quickly, which was strange for the men to see. Sam always meandered; he didn't get in a hurry for anything.

Sam stopped and reached in his shirt pocket for his pack of cigarettes, all the while talking, "You are not going to believe this!" he said, as he put the cigarette in his mouth. The cigarette resting between his lips bounced up and down as he spoke, digging for a lighter in his pockets. "Lock, asshole Lock, is in town right now."

Vin handing Sam a lighter, said, "What?"

"Yeah, the son of a bitch is here." Sam answered, lighting his cigarette, taking a deep inhale, "And he's been here for over a week now." Sam finished blowing a billow of smoke from his lungs.

James put his hand out, "Wait, wait a minute, you mean he was here when Charlie was attacked?"

Sam nodded his head, taking another deep inhale off his cigarette.

James ran his hands over his face and through his hair, "son of a bitch," he said more to himself.

Sam said, "I told him to meet me at the bar tonight at 8. We are all going to go."

Roger broke into the conversation, "wait, we don't have any proof."

Sam interrupted him, "No, it's not like that. I'm going to talk to him. See what he knows about Rylan's death and Charlie's attack." I just want you all there at tables to have my back, just in case."

As the men were thinking about what Sam was saying, Vin was nodding in agreement with Sam, "Yeah, that would work. I mean, look, Sam can take care of himself, but Lock hasn't seen us in years. He might recognize one of us but not all of us. He won't try anything if we are all there." Vin said

Roger said, "OK, I guess that's true."

Sam said, "Look, as soon as I get some info, I'll give you all a signal, and we all head out together."

James said, "Yeah, that way, when it's over, he will know we were there, but he won't know till it's over."

Sam pointed his finger at James, "Exactly."

Vin said, "Well, I'm in."

The guys all agreed they were in. Now they just had to wait for Aaron and keep the information about Lock being in town away from Stacy.

Aaron exited the hospital alone and told the guys Stacy would stay and then go home with Charlie's parents for the night. "She said she'd see y'all tomorrow," Aaron said.

Vin and Sam filled Aaron in about the meeting. Aaron agreed.

The meeting

Aaron, Sam, Farmer, and Vin were all loaded into Aaron's SUV and heading to the bar. James and Roger were going to meet up with them there. Aaron pulled the SUV into a parking spot next to Sam's truck they still had yet to pick up from the bar.

Aaron said, "Farmer, you and Vin go in. I'll come in in a few minutes and join you at your table. Sam, you come in last and take a seat at the bar."

They agreed and started to unload from the SUV. Before Aaron went in, James and Roger pulled up.

Aaron said, "Y'all go get a seat at a table across the room from Vin and Farmer. That way, we will have all the exits covered, just in case he comes in and sees us and tries to leave."

Although this meeting was Sam's idea, Sam was happy to let Aaron take over. He was focused on his conversation with Lock. Sam kept running what he would say through his head. Like we all have done at some point in our life, Sam prepared himself for wherever the conversation would lead. Accept there was information he needed to get from Lock. Sam wanted answers. He needed answers but knew Lock would never tell him if he asked straight out.

Roger and James headed into the bar. Aaron followed about 3 minutes behind them. It was then that Sam noticed someone in the parking lot, sitting in a car parked about four cars down from Aaron's SUV. Sam sat watching, and the man exited his car. Once the man was under the light of the bar's porch, Sam was positive it was Lock.

Sam waited for Lock to go in, and then he walked to the porch of the bar and walked in. He spotted Lock right away sitting on a stool at the bar. So, Sam took a seat next to him.

Sam thought it would be hard for him to be at the bar and not drink, but actually, his mind was totally preoccupied with Lock. He had not given drinking a single thought.

When Sam sat down, Lock did a double-take when he saw Sam. Lock said, "damn, dude, you look like shit. Time has not been your friend."

Sam laughed, keeping his cool, "Yeah, well, this week has been a bitch."

Lock said, "So what do you want? I mean, this place doesn't really appeal to me."

Sam said, "I know. I heard you like those drugged-out whore houses."

"Where did you hear that?" Lock said, not looking at Sam.

"Doesn't matter, I just what to know what you've heard about Rylan's death," Sam said, trying to keep it casual.

"Rylan? Dude, that was years ago. Why you want to dig that up?"

"Because," Sam said, "inquiring minds and all. Plus, I thought you might have a local's perspective."

Lock mulled it over, looking at the bottom of his whiskey glass. "All I know is, she was found in an alley behind a liquor store. Man, who knows, what happened, she was probably trying to score."

"See, that's what I thought at first too, but she was clean. She'd been clean for a year. Not to mention there were no drugs in her system when they did the autopsy." Sam explained.

Lock looked at him suspiciously, "How do you know that?"

"Doesn't matter; I just do." Sam said, "And now I want to know more, like what you heard around town after it happened."

"For the record, I didn't know she was there, but I heard it was ruled accidental because they couldn't prove homicide." Lock spit the words out of his mouth.

Sam put his hands on the bar so Lock could see them. He looked straight into Lock's face and asked, "Was it an accidental Lock, or did you get away with murder."

"What the fuck, Sam? I didn't even know Rylan lived there. As far as I know, she didn't know I lived there either." Lock explained. "You have a big pair to come here and try to accuse me of something."

Sam said, "I have a big pair, that's for sure, but it's not for accusing you of anything. See, I know your lying. I know you and Rylan were hanging out together before she was killed. I also know after she was killed you saw Charlie down in Florida." Sam actually didn't know any of those things. He was bluffing.

Lock said, "No, I didn't. Why would I want to see that bitch."

Sam balled his hands into fists, "I didn't say you wanted to see Charlie. I'm saying you did see her. She confronted you, didn't she?"

Lock smirked, "Yeah, so I did see Charlie. She did come to my house and confront me about Rylan. So, what. I told her the same thing I'm gonna tell you. I didn't see Rylan, and I didn't know she was in Florida, much less the same town as me."

Sam Said, "See, here's the thing, I don't know what you did to Charlie the night she confronted you, but I was the one that came to Florida. I was there. The only reason I don't know what you did is because she didn't tell me. She knew if I had found out about you being there, I'd have killed your mother fucking ass. I was there, Lock, something happened, and when I find out what happened between you and Charlie, I will take you out."

The Bartender put another whiskey in front of Lock, and Lock swigged it down, "Ok," Lock said, looking around the bar, "Let's say Charlie did come to see me after Rylan's funeral. Let's say she told me she had evidence that I had seen Rylan. Let's say she, just like you, thought I had killed Rylan. Let's say I invited Charlie into my car to talk about it, and when she got in the car, I hit that sweet pussy like it was hot apple pie at a fat guy's cookout."

Sam's face burned hot with anger, the pit of his stomach raged with hate, and it was all Sam could do to control himself and keep looking as if he didn't care. On the inside, though, he was ready to rip Lock limb from limb.

Lock continued, "I'm not saying that's what happened but let's just say it did. Why would you care about it? You can't prove anything, and you never will. That was what, almost six years ago?"

Sam said, "Yeah, your probably right. So, have you seen Charlie since you been back to town?"

Lock laughed, "No, good thing too, or they might think I was the one that fucked her up. Hats off to whoever did."

Sam stood up from the barstool and said, "Ok, I really hope I don't see you around." Sam started to walk away, and he looked at the guys and gave a slight nod that it was time to go. Sam stopped behind Lock, leaned over his shoulder, and said, "By the way, if you ever disrespect Charlie, like calling her bitch or give her any type of wrong look, I will cut your balls off and shove them down your fuckin throat." Sam grabbed the back of Lock's shirt, yanked him hard off the Barstool backward, and walked away, leaving Lock on the bar room floor.

The guys all met at the back of Aaron's SUV. Once in the SUV, they rode silently. Finally, Sam broke the silence by saying, "I think Lock killed Rylan, and I think Charlie has a way to prove it." Sam spit the words out fast so he wouldn't stop himself from saying it. He knew it sounded insane. He had no proof he was going on a feeling deep in his guts.

James said, "We would need proof, rock-solid proof, and we can take Lock down for both Charlie's attack and Rylan's death."

Farmer said, "Yeah, but what could she have on him?"

Aaron said, "I don't know, but if it was enough for Lock to come after her, after all this time, it must have been something worth showing up for."

Sam said, "That's true, but what could she have found almost six years later?"

None of them had an answer, and they all sat quietly again. They all got out of Aaron's SUV at Sam's house. They were standing around his deck, listening to Sam's play-by-play of the meeting. Eventually, Aaron took James and Roger back to the Bar to get their car. They left with promises of seeing each other soon.

Sam and Aaron were left in the SUV. Sam was planning on taking his truck back home, but he just sat in Aaron's SUV. He wasn't attempting to get out just yet.

When Sam broke the silence, "Aaron, I have to say something, and it's one of those things no one wants to say aloud."

Aaron just sat there listening to his brother. Then said, "It's cool, bro, whatever it is, you can tell me."

"You can't tell the guys. It's too personal. You have to keep this our secret." Sam explained.

Aaron looked to Sam, "Dude, ok, just spit it out, your kind of freaking me out."

Sam inhaled the night air from the downed window, "I think Lock raped Charlie when she was down in Florida. I think Ryan is Lock's son, not her husband's son."

Aaron inadvertently let off the SUV's gas, reveling in the information. He almost missed a curve, and Sam had to yell his name to snap him back to the present.

Aaron said, "Holy shit! That makes sense! I mean, it's horrible for Charlie, but it makes sense. Ryan, Charlie's son, is the right age, more so than the age from her husband's death. Plus, she wouldn't want anyone to know about Ryan's father, especially if everyone just assumed it was her husband."

Sam continued to look out the window and said, "Yeah, I know, that's what I'm thinking, and although Lock didn't admit anything, it's what he said and the way he said it."

"That would make sense why she called you to come down and pick her up, not want to talk about why she was there or what happened while she was there," Aaron said, and Sam nodded in agreement.

"Yeah, we can't let the guys know about this. This is Charlie's story to tell, not ours." Aaron finished.

Sam finally looked at Aaron, "Is it wrong? That makes me love her even more. She conceived that child in rape and kept it to raise. I mean, I've not seen her in years, but I bet she loves that child more than her life."

Aaron agreed, "She does, I've seen her with him, and Ryan is a great kid."

The phone

The following day Aaron drove to Charlie's parent's house to pick up Stacy. Aaron still had Charlie's phone in his pocket. It weighed heavy when he walked. It was not because the phone was actually heavy, but because he felt there were answers in there and every time he walked and felt the phone hit against his leg, it reminded him that the phone was there. Aaron pulled into the driveway and headed to the door.

Before he could reach the door, Stacy had the screen door wide open and was yelling, "Hurry, come in."

Aaron picked up the pace and entered the house at a run. "The hospital called," Stacy said

Aaron responded, "She's awake?"

Stacy shook her head no, but still smiling when she said, "No, but she was choking on the ventilator, and they had to remove it, which means she is breathing on her own."

Aaron clasps his hands as if he were praying, "That's a good sign, right?" He asked.

"For sure, it means she is healing, and her brain is functioning," Stacy said.

Charlie's mother walked in with Charlie's son Ryan. Aaron greeted her kindly as always, then reached into her pocket and held Charlie's phone out. "Do you know how to unlock this?" He asked. Her mother looked at it but didn't take it, "No, I wouldn't know how to work that fancy phone."
About that time, Ryan grabbed the phone from Aaron's hand, Ryan swiped his pointer finger all over the screen, and the phone chirped. Ryan looked at Aaron and said, "There."

Aaron took the phone and saw it was unlocked. His eyes were wide, and he was in amazement he hadn't thought to ask Ryan sooner.

Aaron looked at Ryan and said, "Thanks, little man, you saved the day again."

Ryan said, "No problem, big dude. Anytime, I'll help you but not John. I never helped him."

Aaron looked at Stacy with a sideways glare and smiled. Stacy shrugged her shoulders, "Kids, they know more about this electronic stuff than we do." Stacy said

When Aaron and Stacy got to the hospital, Arron swiped the phone unlocked again, just like Ryan had shown him. Stacy asked what he was doing. Aaron told her he was just looking around on the phone for contact, if there were people he needed to call. Soon, Stacy noticed that Aaron wasn't in the phone contacts nor was he in the text section of the phone.

"Ok, Aaron, what are you guys up to?" Stacy asked, "You all disappeared last night, and you were super secretive yesterday when I walked in the room."

Aaron lowered the phone and said, Alright, we are looking into Charlie to see what we can find. If it were any one of us, Charlie would invade our privacy to find answers."

Stacy laughed, "Yeah, that's true. Ok, I won't stop you. I just wish I knew something, anything that would be helpful."

"She never talked to you about anyone or anything. Maybe a boyfriend? Or someone bothering her?" Aaron said, trying to fish for information without actually mentioning Lock's name.

Stacy thought for a few minutes, then answered "No," shaking her head vigorously, "she never said anything about that."

"Did she ever come right out and say that she had gotten pregnant before her husband passed away?" Aaron asked carefully.

"No, I just assumed, why? That seems off-topic."

"Sam and I were talking and realized she never told us either. I mean, I'm sure Ryan is her husband's. We just thought it was strange she never has mentioned it to anyone."

"Yeah, but then again, it was a death. No one wants to bring up a painful memory to a pregnant woman." Stacy said, nibbling on her fingernail.

"True, never thought about that part," Aaron said, still scrolling through the phone.

"Wait a minute," Stacy said, "I've never known Charlie to date since her husband passed away, but one of the ladies in her grief counseling group suggested some website called Chatters.com."

"Chatters.com? what the hell is that." Aaron asked.

Stacy was still looking at her fingernail and trying to scrape a rough edge off the top, "I don't know," she said, "Some platform where you find people in the same tragic situation as you and talk about it. Like a support group, only there are men and women in there."

Aaron flipped the phone's screen to the home screen, and there it was Chatters.com icon.

"Look," Aaron said, pointing to the icon on the home screen.

"Oh my God, she did it! She was on Chatters." Stacy said with a giggle.

Aaron clicked to open the app, and when it pulled up, Charlie had her username and password saved in the request bar.

"Well, thank you, Charlie Rae," Aaron said out loud.

He looked through the app and found the inbox. There was only one message that had been unopened. Aaron clicked to read it. The message read,
"Hey Chatter, we miss you! You have not logged into your account for nine months. Have you found a special someone? Let us know how you are doing."

It was signed 'the staff at chatters.'

"Hum, well, she hasn't been on here in at least seven months, maybe longer," Aaron told Stacy.

Stacy was curious and more out of curiosity than investigation. She said, "Weeellll, maybe we should just look in the app and see if there are any people she talked to regularly."

Arron side-eyed her and said, "I am already looking."

Stacy giggled and said, "Look to see if there is a blocked list. If there is, maybe, we can talk to them and see if there was anyone she had an issue with."

Aaron flipped the screen to the list of options, "Good idea."

Stacy shifted her position in the car's seat now and leaned in to see what Aaron was doing.

Aaron said, "There's only one person on the blocked list. I guess it's a screen name, Redmen."

"Hum, if it works like a dating app, which, let's face it, this seems like a dating app, then you can click the screen name, and it should take you to any conversation she had with Redmen," Stacy added.

Aaron clicked on Redmen, and it took them to a profile and a chat Charlie had with him. "Look," Aaron said, "She gave him her phone number, but it's the phone number to her old phone. At least that's not the number I used in the past to contact her."

Stacy looked at the number, "Yeah, that was the number I had for her before she switched."

Aaron asked, "Did she say why she switched."

Stacy said, "No, just that she needed to lose some contacts off the old number. But she said it jokingly, so I didn't think anything of it."

"We need to get that old phone back," Aaron said and pulled his phone out of his pocket to call Charlie's mother.

Vin and Charlie

Vin was staying at Aaron's house while he was in town. He'd gone to his mother's house and visited. Now he was back at Aaron's lying on the couch. Aaron was out with Stacy, and they were planning to stay at the hospital for the night. Vin knew Aaron would not have alcohol in his house, so he stopped to get a small bottle of Jack but left the liquor store with a large bottle of Jack Daniels. He'd poured himself a drink and walked out to the back deck to enjoy the country air, which he didn't get much of at his city Studio.

After calling his wife, he laid on the couch, but he couldn't get settled. The image of Charlie lying in the hospital keeps creeping back into his mind. This memory leads to all the things the guys had been finding out about her past. He felt like the pieces of the puzzle were there, but he just couldn't seem to make them fit. He walked back to the kitchen and poured himself another drink, then went to sit on the deck again. He sat in a lounge chair and kicked his legs up. Starting to feel the effects of the whiskey, he tilted his head back and looked up at the stars. His fuzzy brain begun to bring forth a memory of Charlie. Her face in his face, the moon rising behind her. Charlie's hair was blowing. The clouds seemed to move in fast forward overhead, but Charlie's image was in slow motion.

They were young, only sophomores in high school. They had been fighting with each other since the beginning of school. The school year was already about to break for Thanksgiving. They had been arguing so much that the guys didn't even want to be around them. Sam, who usually was always up for hanging out, had stopped joining them all together.

One Friday night, Farmer picked Aaron, Vin, and Charlie up, and they met up with Roger and James down by the old train bridge. They all were hanging out, making plans for the weekend when Vin and Charlie started arguing again. Aaron and Farmer got in Farmer's truck without a word, and Roger and James got in Roger's truck and took off, leaving Vin and Charlie there. On the way out, Aaron yelled, "Figure the hell out what y'all's problem is. We can't stand it anymore."

Angry, Charlie started blaming Vin and Vin began blaming Charlie. After they had yelled all they could think of to yell at each other, Charlie began walking towards town.

Completely annoyed by the situation, Vin yelled, "Where are you going?"

Charlie stopped and said, "Well, I'm not staying here with you all night. I'm walking home."

"Hold on. You can't walk alone. I'm coming too." Vin said.

Charlie looked at Vin and laughed sarcastically, "Really, Vin, I can't go alone? I can do whatever I want."

Reaching for Charlie's arm, Vin said, "Charlie, you know, that's not what I meant."

"Really? What did you mean, you think I'm just some girl?" Charlie said.

"Oh! I know you're a girl, but you're not just some girl." Vin said. Charlie looked at Vin, exasperated. Her eyes were burning a hole in Vin's face. Vin continued, "Damn Charlie. You're beautiful. You break my heart every day." Charlie's eyes began to soften. "Charlie, you're all I can think about, all day, every day. I just want to hold you and kiss you." Charlie walked closer to Vin. His arms were to his sides, and she put her hands on his arms and ran them down to his hands.

"What's going on, Vin?" She asked.

He shook his head, "I think I accidentally fell in love with you somewhere along the way."

Charlie stepped into Vin and put her face up to his. He leaned down, and his lips gently touched Charlie's lips. She had never been kissed before, but she couldn't imagine any other first kiss being that perfect. They walked down the road hand in hand. Eventually, Vin suggested they lay down in Johnson's field, which was right off the road. So, they walked about 50 feet into the field. Vin laid his flannel shirt down on the ground, leaving him with only his tee-shirt. They both laid on the shirt and looked up at the stars. Charlie leaned over Vin while he lay on his back. She looked him in the face. The stars were shining as the autumn moon was rising behind her. Vin could see her shining blue eyes, even in the dark, as she laughed and giggled at his jokes.

They dated for nearly a year. Charlie didn't know what she was supposed to feel. She didn't know what love was. She liked Vin. She liked having a boy-friend. The boy that was also her friend, made things so easy for her. However, in the middle of their junior year of high school, Charlie and Vin had broken off the relationship. Ultimately, their love was one of friendship, and they knew it. They had been confused by teenage angst and hormones. When Charlie was contemplating her virginity, she had considered asking Vin but knew that was a bad idea because of their history. Then things had happened with Sam, and she was happy with her decision. Just as her first kiss felt perfect, her first sexual experience had felt perfect. Just as Sam had promised, no one ever found out about their summer or what they had done.

Vin lay on the deck lounger now, wishing Charlie were there to laugh about the past. Vin loved his wife, but he would never forget Charlie. Vin stumbled into the house and lay on the couch, where he fell into an uneasy drunken sleep. The following day, Vin woke to the sun shining and the birds chirping. They made him angry, the sun shouldn't be shinning, and the birds shouldn't be happily chirping their songs.

Vin showered and dressed and headed to the hospital. When he opened the hospital door to Charlie's room, he found Sam next to Charlie, not Aaron and Stacy. Vin asked where they were. Sam didn't know, he had gotten there last night, and Charlie was alone in the room. Sam decided to stay until Aaron and Stacy returned, but they hadn't. Vin was surprised that Aaron would leave Charlie alone but was glad Sam had been there. Vin offered to stay so Sam could go home and rest, but Sam refused. The two of them sat in Charlie's room watching her sleep.

Present Aaron and Stacy

Aaron and Stacy had met Charlie's mother at the hospital to get the old cell phone. They went and rented a room in the only hotel in Harriston, so Stacy would have a place to rest other than Charlie's parent's house. The hotel was a hole in the wall and hadn't been updated since the '80s and was in desperate need of new carpet, bedding, and tile. But the sheets were clean, and the bathroom smelled of bleach, so they assumed it must be cleaner than it looked.

Aaron had called James and told him Stacy and himself had the phones, and they may be on to something but didn't know what yet. Aaron and Stacy reviewed the information on the phones over carryout food and sodas. The phone revealed that Charlie and Redmen had texted back and forth for several months. But they were at a loss as to what Redmen's real name was. It did seem as if Charlie had, on at least one occasion, met up with Redmen.

They decided to break from the phones and rest for a few hours with their bellies full of fast food and sodas. They lay next to each other on their back, covers pulled up to their armpits, not touching each other. Aaron's heart was beating a million beats per minute. He used to dream about having Stacy alone in a hotel room. Now they were here, and he was too afraid to touch her. He'd thought of using some of his brother's smooth, easy pickup lines. They always seemed to work for Sam but then abandoned that thought after he saw Stacy laying there. The light shining through a crack in the curtains and fell perfectly on Stacy's face. Besides, he liked Stacy, and Sam's lines were usually used on drunken one-night stands.

Then he began to think about Sam. He realized; he didn't know who his brother was anymore. He wasn't the same drunken, always looking for a good time, Sam anymore. Sam had changed, just like Aaron had changed. Aaron vowed that he would get to know his brother better and make a more profound effort to have him in his life again.

Stacy spoke, pulling Aaron from his thoughts, "What's on your mind, your quiet."

Aaron sort of pushed a laugh out and said, "This situation is strange. I've always wanted to be in a room alone with you, and now here we are."

Stacy agreed it was strange. "So, what did you think about when you wanted to have me in a room alone?" She asked.

Aaron hesitated. He almost said, 'I can tell you, or I can just show you, but instead, he fumbled out words to string together a sentence. "Well, I don't think I should say. It may not be exactly gentlemanly."

Stacy turned to her side, facing Aaron, and said, "Then just show me instead of telling me."

Aaron laughed inside a little at the similarity of her words to his thoughts. Taken aback a little by her forwardness, but he did not hesitate to make his move at her signal. He leaned towards her and put his hand behind her neck. Stacy moved her head so that Aaron's hand cradled her head. He firmly pulled her close to him and kissed her deeply. From there, they let their impulse do the rest of the work.

Aaron was in the bathroom the following day, and Stacy was still lying in bed, in only her bra. Her brain was trying to work through something. She sat up in the bed to clear her mind, then asked Aaron, "Did we read the messages in Chatters? The one's Charlie and Redmen wrote to each other before Charlie gave him her phone number."

Aaron called from the bathroom, "probably, we read them all. I can't remember?"

Still trying to figure out the connection, she said, "I didn't think of this before, but maybe he told her his name in one of those messages."

Stacy pulled the old phone out and started clicking through the messages. He hadn't told her his name, but he gave her his phone number. Stacy didn't know why that excited her, because they knew his phone number from the old phone.

Aaron had returned from the bathroom and was sitting on the bed next to Stacy, looking at the phone.

He said, "Yeah but look. There is a time gap. See," and he pointed to the messages. Stacy looked and reread the messages.

"Yeah, your right. There is like a four-month gap where they didn't message on Chatters."

They continued to read the messages on the Chatters app.

"Stacy said, "Is it just me being a woman, or did the tone of her messages change when Redmen started talking to her again, after that gap."

Aaron read them in sequence and said, "No, I think your right. When I read this before, I thought she was talking about meeting him. See here she says, 'No, I won't.' That's not about a meeting."

Stacy and Aaron wrote down the phone number down given to Charlie in the messages and compared it to the old phone's phone number. It wasn't the same.

"Oh my gosh, Aaron, they aren't the same. They are similar but not the same." Stacy said, pulling out the new phone.

She swiped it unlocked like Ryan had shown them the day before and started to scroll through the contacts looking for a number that matched the one given in the Chatter's messages.

"Here it is!" She exclaimed.

Aaron stopped reading and grabbed the phone from Stacy, "Who does it belong to?"

They both stopped breathing for a second and looked at each other with astonishment, "Johnny," they both said at the same time.

A Call to Arms

Stacy and Aaron both dressed quickly and got into the car to head to the hospital. Aaron called everyone and told them to meet him at the hospital. Sam was already there, but everyone else agreed they'd meet there. Vin was on his way to lunch from the hospital, but he rushed through a drive-through and hurried back. Sam came out of Charlie's room, and they all met in the second-floor lobby. It all felt very familiar, just a day before they'd been in the same place all together again for the first time in nearly 18 years.

The guys were all standing around in the lobby, and Stacy now joined them. Aaron and Stacy had a look on their faces like they were keeping a secret, which everyone assumed were about to be revealed. Finally, Roger said, "Ok, what's going on?"

All the guys now standing in a huddle facing Aaron and Stacy agreed and were visibly anxious. Aaron started with the phones and explained how the old phone Farmer found wasn't a bust after all. Then, Stacy broke in and started explaining how the new phone fit into the puzzle and what they had seen on the new phone.

James stopped them and asked, "So what does any of this have to do with Lock."

The guys looked at James, and Stacy looked at Aaron. Stacy was visibly taken aback by hearing Lock's name.

Aaron looked to Stacy and put his hand out to reassure her, "No, Stacy, it's alright." Aaron said. Stacy was upset, "What about Lock? Why is he in this? You all are keeping secrets from me now." She said.

Aaron trying to calm her down, said, "No!, It's not like that." Stacy turned towards the elevator and punched the down button.

"Stacy, don't leave," Aaron said.

The guys all joined in, "Don't go, we can explain." Stacy loaded onto the elevator without saying another word to any of them.

Farmer told Aaron, "You should go after her." Aaron deflated, answered, "I will. She can't get far; I have the keys." He said, holding his index finger up and shaking the keys as the ring was hanging around his finger. "First, I need you to know what I found." He finished as he slid the keys back in his pocket.

Quickly Aaron told them he didn't think Lock had anything to do with the attack. He thought he might have something to do with Rylan's death, but that would be for another day.

Aaron said, "Long story short, we don't think Charlie gave this Redmen person her new number. We think she got the new number to avoid him. But we can't prove any of that till Charlie wakes up but more importantly, Stacy and I figured out that Redmen is actually a guy named John. We looked through Charlie's phone, and she has a contact in her phone named Johnny."

James said, "How do you know that John or Johnny is Redmen?"

Aaron said, "When I was at Charlies' parent's house, Ryan opened the phone for me. He said he never helped John open the phone."

The guys all had an ah-ha moment at the same time.

Then Vin said, "So you think this Redmen, Johnny person was seeing Charlie and it didn't end well, maybe? So maybe, he had something to do with this?"

Aaron was shaking his head yes. Roger cut in, "Well, it's a lead for sure. If nothing else, maybe he could tell us something else we don't know."

Aaron said, "Ok, well, hold up, we don't know Johnny's last name, and it isn't Redmen. We already checked. The people from the website won't release any names without a court order."

James said, "Yeah, you won't get a court order off what we have. Mostly, it's all speculation, but it really is a good lead."

Roger said, "Hold on! I might have something that will help." He pulled his phone out and started scrolling and punching buttons frantically. The guys all stood around, looking curiously at him.

Finally, Roger looked up at Aaron, "What's the last number you had for him?" Aaron gave it to him, and Roger put it in his phone.

Vin said, "Guys, why don't we just call the number and ask him what his last name is? You know, like is this John Smith, and he will say no, this is John Whatever."

Aaron said, "We tried that. It's disconnected."

James said, "That's not a good sign. The phone number is disconnected."

They all looked at James, and James explained, "People don't normally disconnect phone numbers unless they are running from bill collectors or they have committed a crime and the crime is linked with the phone."

Farmer said, "Well, that certainly applies in this case."

Roger said, "I got it!" they all looked at him, and he said, turning his phone around for them to see, "John Butler. See?"

James said, "Holy crap."

Sam clapped his hands, "Hell yeah, now what?"

"Well, I don't know. I mean, we have to connect him to it. If he did it." Aaron Asked, looking at James

James said, "Let me get back to the courthouse, Aaron go take care of Stacy. Sam, you stay here with Charlie. Farmer, Roger, Vin, you all get back to Charlie's place. Don't touch anything, use gloves or something but see what you can find. Anything at this point, a thread, button, spit, I don't know. We need something."

They all agreed and went their separate ways to accomplish the tasks they had been assigned. The truth was none of them knew what they were doing. However, it was a distraction from what they were feeling, making them feel like they were helping. If any of the men were honest, they all felt guilty for not being closer to their friend for so many years.

Courthouse

James entered the lobby of the courthouse, which smelled of old, aged wood and janitorial cleaner. The walls were yellowed with time, but this is where James called home from 9-5, 5 to 6 days a week. He took the stairs two at a time to the second floor, where all the attorneys had offices. James put the key in his office door. He took a seat behind his desk and powered up the computer. He opened a web browser and hit the favorites bar on his browser. He looked for the county arrest records link that held all the records for county criminals. However, this time when it asked what county, he didn't choose his local county as he usually did. He searched through the list and highlighted the counties surrounding Harriston.

James entered the name 'John Butler,' rubbed his hands together, and said to the computer, "Alright baby, what do you have for me today." Then hit the enter button. The computer's brain sprang to life. It clicked and turned inside and then started to produce results. Twenty results popped up. Some were duplicates so he could eliminate those, which left 12 actual results. James read through the digital pages and was able to eliminate seven more based on age. He knew it would be a possibility this guy may not be in the system. However, he felt like this was the guy that had attack Charlie. It was just a gut feeling. No one starts their criminal career attacking a woman while her child is in the next room. He felt confident he would find a record of this John Butler.

James was scrolling through the five remaining records of possible subjects when he reached the second to last, he froze. "I've seen this guy before." He mumbled to the empty office. He clicked the 'read more' option, and the full record popped open. James starred at the mugshot on the screen. The man in the photo glared back at him. The mugshot was dark, and the man's hair was messy. His eyes were bloodshot, and he had a busted lip. Still, James was sure he'd seen him before. James was trying to recover the memory of where he'd seen him. James was in deep concentration, out of habit; he reached for his coffee cup that always sat on the edge of his desk. When he pulled it to his mouth, it was, of course empty, he returned it to the edge of the desk. "Coffee," James shouted to the picture on the computer, "I saw you at the coffee shop in town. You're the guy that made an ass of himself at the coffee shop." James hovered his mouse over the option and clicked the 'AKA' option. James almost lost his mind. The screen read, "John Butler also known as Johnny Butler, also known as Redmen."

James, under his breath, said, "You're a moron." and clicked the print record button. As James waited for the pages to print, he read the screen which detailed his charges. The charges included DUI, domestic violence, and possession of drug paraphernalia. "Oh, Charlie, what have you gotten into," James said to the computer screen. James knew there was no way she could have known any of this. James grabbed the printed pages off the printer and ran towards his car, dialing whomever he could reach first. Sam, still sitting in the hospital room with Charlie, answered first. James yelled into the phone, "I got him!" Once James got into his car, he took a picture of the printout and forwarded it to all the guys in a group text message with the words, "gotta love technology," attached to the text.

Charlie's House

Farmer let himself into the window the way he had entered Charlie's house the first time he was there. All the guys had in the car were winter gloves, but they were wearing them now and felt stupid with winter gloves on in the middle of summer. Once in the house, Farmer unlocked the back door and let Vin and Roger in. They started searching for anything that shouldn't have been there. The problem was none of them had been to Charlie's house except for Farmer a few days before, and Aaron had come to see her recently. However, Aaron and Stacy were missing in action again.

"Some of that blood has to be his. I mean, there is no way Charlie wouldn't have fought back with her son in the next room." Vin said.

Roger agreed, "Yeah, but the problem is testing it all. I mean, if that's the only way, we could try to get the police to do that, but it would take months."

Farmer agreed, "If we don't find anything concrete, then that's what we will have to do."

They walked around the house through the kitchen, around the living room, looking under furniture and shelves but weren't finding anything specific. Farmer flipped on the hall light, looked to see Charlie's room, and opened the door to Ryan's room.

Farmer asked, "They said that the guy put Ryan in his room and then locked him in there, right?"

Vin yelled from the living room, "Yes, I think that's what they said."

"I see the chair he used to lock the bedroom door." Farmer said as he continued into Ryan's room.

Farmer looked around the room and found toys on the floor. It looked like Ryan was trying to play with them while he was locked in there. Then he found a box of crayons on the floor next to a book of blank paper and saw where Ryan had been coloring. He'd drawn a picture of a man with red hair. His mother was in the picture. It looked like she was lying on the couch. Then it looked like Ryan had scribbled an "X" through the man with red hair. Farmer looked through the rest of the pictures Ryan had drawn, but that was the only one with the red-haired man.

Farmer took the page and ripped it out of the notebook, "Hey, look at this." Farmer said, walking into the living room. Vin emerged from Charlie's room, and Roger was on all fours in the living room looking under a bookshelf.

Looking at the picture, they were silent. Finally, Vin said, "That's creepy." They all agreed it was creepy, and the picture had to mean something. Farmer folded it up and put it in his pants pocket. Roger shook off a cold chill that ran up his spine. They looked around the house for another 30 minutes or so and then decided to leave. When they got into the car Roger said, "Does Charlie have a Dog?"

Vin said, "I don't think so. I think it died like last year or something."

"Hum, I got dog hair all over my pants when I was on the ground looking under the shelves," Roger explained and finished. "See," he said, showing them the dog hair he was picking off his pants.

Vin said, "That's weird. It's white. Her dog was black. Plus, it's been gone for a while. I remember Aaron telling me he helped her bury it."

Farmer said, "That almost looks like bunny hair. Maybe she got Ryan a bunny, and it took off. You know bunnies don't last long out here in the sticks."

They all agreed and rode back to the hospital in silent contemplation.

Aaron and Stacy

James was already back at the hospital with Sam when Vin, Farmer, and Roger walked in. Sam asked if they had found anything?

Farmer said, "No, not really. Only this picture." Farmer showed it to them, saying, "I think Ryan drew it."

Sam Said, "Oh, that's creepy, but according to Charlie's mother, the police asked Ryan if he knew who had locked him in the room, and he said he didn't know who it was."

James said, "Yeah, but he also first said he didn't know how he got in the room. Then he changed it and said he was locked in there. The police didn't think he was reliable. At least that's what the report indicated."

"Ok, but what if Ryan did know but didn't know how to tell the police. I mean, that would be a lot for a five-year-old to handle." Vin suggested

Sam interjected, "Poor kid, he probably was scared shitless."

James said, "I don't know. Is this something we could ask Ryan?"

"I wouldn't bring it up if you didn't have to. Maybe ask Charlie's mother if Ryan had said anything else to them." Sam suggested.

Farmer excused himself from the room and called Charlie's mother. The guys couldn't hear what was said, but they could hear Farmer agreeing with whomever he was talking to.

About 20 minutes later, Farmer came back into the room and said, "Well, Ryan did talk to Charlie's mother. They didn't take it to the police because Ryan still never identified a specific person. But get this, Ryan told Charlie's parents, after having a nightmare one night, the man looked like Johnny, but it didn't look like Johnny." Sam and Roger's heads both jerked up to attention.

James said, "I know, but they didn't tell the police because they think Johnny is a character in a TV show. They said they don't know a Johnny, so we think he is confusing something he saw on TV with reality."

Sam said, "Could be, kids are strange that way, but that would be a hell of a coincidence don't you think."

They agreed. Then Sam asked, "Has anyone heard from Aaron and Stacy? I mean, my god, it's obvious they did the deed the other night, but can't they wait? There are more pressing issues at hand."

Vin and Roger laughed and both said they hadn't heard from either of them.

Farmer said, "Damn, Sam, you have such a way with words."

Not sure what to do with the current information they had. They all just sat there discussing options. Occasionally one of them would look at Charlie as if to ask her if she could give her input. However, unfortunately, she never responded.

Sam put his hand on hers and squeezed a little, "It's ok, Charlie girl, just rest and get better. When you wake, we will have this all fixed up for you, I promise." Sam told her, desperately wishing she would squeeze his hand back, but again, she didn't.

Sam had gone down the hall to use the restroom and get a bite to eat. While Farmer and Vin stayed in the room with Charlie. Roger and James had left for their homes, and Vin and Farmer were going to leave when Sam returned. Sam was sitting in the second-floor lobby eating and lying on the lobby's couch when the elevator dinged to announce a passenger's arrival. He watched as Aaron and Stacy ran off the elevator towards Charlie's room. They were in such a hurry they didn't even see Sam sitting there. Curious, Sam got up and followed behind them. They entered the room, and Sam came in behind them.

Sam asked Aaron in a whisper, "Where the hell you two been? This isn't the time to go disappear on us."

Aaron said breathless, "We didn't. We went to do some recon."

Sam laughed under his breath, "Recon my ass," Sam said quietly and rolled his eyes. He was about to give Aaron an earful.

Farmer looked at them crazy, "Recon? What do you mean?"

Aaron was scrolling through his phone while Stacy tried to fill them in, "That picture James sent to us, it had the guy's address on it, so we thought we'd just drive by to see if he still lived there."

Vin said, "Holy shit Aaron what were you thinking?"

Aaron looked at Vin, "I was thinking I was going to see what this guy knew, and I was going to find out one way or another." Aaron said.

Sam said, "Well, what's done is done? So, what did you see?"

Aaron turned his phone around and said, "He still lives there, and Charlie beat the shit out of him before he got her. See, she broke his nose; he has two black eyes, and she scratched him down both arms." Aaron showed them the picture.

Stacy interrupted, "So, He came out walking this tiny little furball, and I jumped out of the car and acted like I was walking around the block. And when I passed him, I said hello, you know, as a neighbor would. Then I said, oh gosh! all dramatic like, what happened to your face." She said in a fake friendly voice, reenacting her experience. She laughed and continued, "Best performance of my life, anyway, he said he fell and hit his face. So, I say, oh! You scratched your arms too. Did the dog do that? And he just nodded and walked off. Like he didn't want to talk about it anymore. I mean, would you want to talk about it if you got beat up by a girl."

Aaron looked at Stacy and said, "Stacy, you've had too much coffee, chill a minute." Aaron told them that what Stacy had done was not ideal, but she did snap a closeup of his face and time-stamped it. "I think we should take this to the police."

Once Aaron and Stacy stopped talking for half a second, long enough for someone else to get a word in.

Vin said, "Did you say he was walking a fur ball dog?"

Stacy and Aaron both nodded.

"Was it white?" Farmer asked?

They both nodded yes.

Vin said, "Son of bitch, we got him."

Only Vin, Roger, and Farmer knew what was going on. Roger wasn't there, but Vin and Farmer were celebrating with high fives and man hugs. So, Farmer explained to the rest of the group.

A quiet fell across the tiny hospital room as they all took in what had just happened. When they set out to find who had hurt their friend, they had done so out of hurt, fear, and anger; they didn't think they would actually find the guy. To all of their disbelief, they had. Now they didn't know what to do with the information.

Sam said, "I'm here with Charlie till morning. I think we should all separate and go home. Let's take some time and think about what we want to do with this information."

Farmer looked at Sam, "Man, what has happened to you. That's a solid idea, but totally unlike you to come up with it. Normally you would announce it was proof enough for you and go after him."

Sam looked at Farmer as if to say, who me. With a half-smirk on his face.

Farmer continued, "I don't mean no disrespect, I just mean normally you'd been out the door already headed to beat the shit out of the guy."

Sam laughed a genuine laugh and smiled. He said, "Well yeah, but I'm turning over new leaves."

The men seemed genuinely impressed with Sam's newfound restraint. They also took Sam's advice.

Sam-Breaking Point

They all went to their homes for the night, and Sam tried to get as comfortable as he could in the stiff hospital recliner chair and tried to catch a few winks before morning. He couldn't sleep thinking about the image of the man on his phone. He flipped his phone open and glared at the man in the arrest photo James had texted them.
His heart was thudding in his chest, and anger was boiling in his veins. He stood to his feet purposefully. He leaned down and kissed Charlie on the forehead. He lingered there for a moment and whispered, "I'm sorry, sweet Charlie girl, I have to go, but I'll be back soon."

He headed to the elevator but stopped at the nurse's station on his way out. The girl at the station said, "Hey Sam? You here to see Charlie?" He looked at her with a familiar stare when her face came to mind. He said, "Oh hey, I didn't know you worked here."

She smiled and said," I haven't seen you since high school graduation. That was a great party you threw that night."

His face reddened, remembering his graduation party and all the ridiculous things he did. He said. "Yeah, that was something. Listen, I have to step out for a bit. It's probably unlikely, but if Charlie does wake up can you call me?" he said, jotting down his phone number for her.

She said, "Sure," and before she could finish her sentence, Sam was already walking away. He walked with his hands in his pockets but with a purpose, not his normal relaxed stride.

Inside Sam's truck, he was armed with John Butler's picture, address, and a 38. He was determined to make things right, no matter the cost. Sam pulled the gear shift of the old truck into drive and said to the empty truck, "I haven't turned over that many new leaves yet," And headed to the city to make things right.

Sam's truck window was all the way down. The summer air filled the cab of the truck. His thoughts wandered as the miles passed under his tires. He tried not to think about Charlie and focused on what he had found out about Lock and Rylan. Rylan didn't deserve what happened to her, he thought to himself. However, the thought of Rylan lead to the thoughts of Charlie, and slowly Sam began to remember his time with Charlie. The time he went to Florida to pick her up after Rylan's funeral.

Charlie had been vague about the situation. She had called and asked Sam to please come get her. When he questioned why she was still in Florida when the funeral had been over for nearly two weeks, Charlie shut down all his questions and pleaded with him to come to get her. He, of course, threw some clothes in a duffle bag and headed to Florida that night.

When he'd gotten to Florida and found Charlie's hotel, she was waiting for him in the parking lot. Without a word, she handed her suitcase to Sam, and she put her stuff in the back of the truck. Sam looked at Charlie and said, "not a hello, thanks or fuck you?"
Charlie looked at Sam and leaned into him for a hug. The hug started very cold, but as Sam hugged Charlie, she began to melt; she broke down, and it was all she could do to stand. Sam stood there holding Charlie, supporting her weight to help her stand, and let her cry until she stopped. Without a word, they got into Sam's truck and started to head home. Sam didn't know what had happened, but he knew it must have been terrible for Charlie to react that way.

Neither of them were in a hurry to get back, and they spent the next three weeks traveling the states on the way back to Harriston. At times Charlie was cold and distant. Other times she was angry and wandered off to be alone. But most of the time spent, that three weeks, was in Sam's arms crying. She would fall asleep crying, wake crying and cry in her dreams. Sam didn't say hardly anything. He only supported her by listening when she did actually want to talk.

Mid trip, they had stopped at the beach in South Carolina. Charlie had almost seemed her usual self for the moment. Sam didn't think it would last, so he was enjoying the moment. His truck was backed up to the beach. The tailgate down, and he and Charlie were laying in the back. They were watching the sun go down over the water, with their backs leaned against the cab of the truck. Charlie had on a thin cotton dress that kept blowing in the beach wind. Without warning, Charlie sat up and said, "I'm going swimming." She hopped out of the truck bed and began to run to the water. Sam sat up and watched her. When he realized she was actually going to do it, He called after her, "Wait for me."

Charlie began to pull her dress off almost to the water, revealing only her underwear and thin cotton bra. She ran into the water still at full speed until she couldn't run anymore. Sam stopped running momentarily to watch her, admiring her in every way. Not just the beauty of Charlie's naked body but also her ambition and determination to enjoy every moment to the fullest even in this tragically horrific time in her life. Her impulsive tendencies to throw caution to the wind at the most appropriate times were what he admired about her the most. Sam dropped his shorts on the beach, revealing his completely naked body as he entered the water slowly and caught up with Charlie. She laughed, with her head thrown back and her mouth in a wide smile at the fact that Sam was totally nude. That laugh reminded Sam of their summer spent in his Jeep driving the back roads of Harriston.

They stood there in the water letting the waves sway them as the water headed onto the shore. Charlie faced Sam and said, "Thank you. Thank you for everything you have ever done for me. But mostly, Thank you for this."

Sam moved in closer to her and put his hand on her waist, "Charlie, I'd do anything for you. All you have to do is ask." He said, leaning down to hold her against him.

Charlie wrapped her arms around Sam, and he looked down at her. He started in for a kiss and then stopped and asked, "Can I?" Charlie didn't answer; she just leaned up to him, and their lips met in the middle. Sam looped his thumbs through Charlie's panties and pulled them down. Charlie let the water wash them out to sea and wrapped her legs around Sam. Sam placed both his hands on Charlie's bottom as they kissed. He entered her for the second time in their life. Charlie flexed and released her legs muscles around Sam's waist, allowing him to move inside her. Their kisses were fast, hard, and deep, so different than the first time they had made love. As they climaxed, Sam still inside Charlie, Charlie arched her back away from Sam to embrace the entire fullness of him. Her nipples were showing through her cotton bra. Sam was overwhelmed with the sight of Charlie enjoying him so completely.

Eventually, they made their way back to the beach, dressed, and returned to the truck bed, where Sam pulled a blanket from behind the truck seat and covered them with it. They slept there until morning where they made love again and then hit the road to head home. The next day Charlie returned to her sullen state. Sam knew, in his mind, it was no reflection on him. However, his heart was breaking to see her completely falling apart again. The crying, rage, and anger, then frustration started all over again. Sam, once again, was patient with her and let her run the gamete of emotions.

They were nearly home, and Sam had asked Charlie if she was ready to get home or if she wanted to stay gone longer. Sam had trickily gotten out of work on a fake medical release and knew he'd have to get back soon. He was willing to risk it a little longer if Charlie wanted to. However, she told him she could handle home now, and so they continued towards Harriston. Two days before the trip ended, Sam noticed slight changes in Charlie, good changes, encouraging signs that she was on the mend. When they pulled into Harriston late one evening, Charlie was smiling and had been talking without bursting into tears. Sam was relieved to see her, the real Charlie, coming back again.

Unfortunately, once home, Sam got into his own head and stopped talking to Charlie altogether. He knew it was a mistake, but he told himself that Charlie was better now. She didn't need him. He told himself, anyone would lose their mind after losing a husband and their best lifelong friend, and now that her heart and head were back on the mend, Charlie would be better without him. He told himself she needed someone but not him. Someone better than him.

What really sealed the deal for Sam was, a few months after they had returned, he'd heard that Charlie and her husband were having a baby. Everyone talked about how wonderful it was that although her husband was gone, she would still have him in the form of his child. It was at that point that Sam lost all control of his drinking. He was happy for her but realized he needed to stay away. The next several years for Sam were filled with work, drinking, meaningless one night stands, and hungover Sundays trying to cope with what was left of his life.

Now it was nearly two AM, and Sam was pulling from the interstate into the city. He followed his GPS to the address listed on the arrest record. Sam pulled up to the front of the house and turned the truck off. There he sat with his truck window down, smoking a cigarette, and waited.

The Awakening

Aaron and Stacy had come to the hospital early the following day to relieve Sam, but Sam wasn't there when they arrived. Aaron and Stacy were nearly done with their drive-through breakfast when James walked into the room. He stated that Charlie's mother was coming soon, but he wanted to spend some time with Charlie before she got there. Aaron and Stacy didn't want to leave. To give James time alone with Charlie, they left and walked to the second-floor lobby. They were talking when the elevator dinged the, now familiar, ding. When the doors opened, Charlie's mother stepped out. Stacy said to Charlie's mother, James was spending some time with Charlie before he had to go to the courthouse, so Charlie's mother sat with them and joined their conversation.

As they were talking, they heard a commotion in the hall, but it was a hospital, so they paid no attention to this at first. Then nurses started running to the room and called over the loudspeaker for a doctor. They looked at one another, and Aaron said, "I'll just be nosy and look around the corner." As he meandered over to the corner of the lobby, he saw James dart from the nurse's station back to Charlie's room, then back to the nurse's station. His arms were flailing wildly, and he was trying to point and talk to everyone. Aaron looked back at the women still sitting in the lobby. Without a word, Aaron took off running like a deer on the side of the road, frightened by an unexpected passing car.

The women, confused as to what just happened, stood and took off behind Aaron. When Aaron arrived in Charlie's room, James was standing over her, his phone was out, and he was recording.

James said, "She hasn't spoken yet, but we think she may be trying to wake up."

Aaron rushed to Charlie's bedside and grabbed her hand. She was blinking rapidly, but her eyes were vacant. She was trying to swallow, but her throat was too dry. Aaron leaned in close to her and whispered, "Charlie, can you hear me? It's Aaron." But Charlie didn't respond.

Stacy and Charlie's mother came running into the room, and Charlie's mother stood at the other side of the bed. James moved to the foot of the bed, still recording. Charlie's mother leaned in close to Charlie's ear. With her gentle, sweet voice, she said, "Charlie, it's Mother." Charlie's eyes were still closed, but she stopped wiggling and turned her head to her mother's voice.

Charlie whispered, "Butt" in the direction of her mother.

Aaron and her mother looked strangely at one another; their eyebrows furrowed in confusion.

Stacy whispered to Aaron, "What did she say? Did she say Butt?" Stacy finished saying hesitantly. Thinking surely that wasn't what she said.

Charlie's mother, still close to Charlie's face, said, "Baby, what did you say?"

Charlie's voice was dry and raspy, but she repeated her whisper, "Butt."

Aaron looked to James, and James looked from behind the phone camera at Aaron.

Aaron said, "Charlie? It's Aaron."

Charlie turned her head to Aaron, her eyes were still closed, but a slight smile turned at the corner of her mouth. She opened her mouth and whispered again, "Butt."

Aaron said, "Charlie, shake your head yes if the person that hurt you was John or Johnny Butler."

Charlie's eyes were closed, but she squeezed them closed even tighter. A tear formed in her closed eyes and slide down her cheek, and she shook her head yes.

Aaron looked at Stacy, "Call Sam!"

Charlie's mother yelled, "Someone call Sam!" Her demanding motherly tone caused the entire room to jump into action again.

James clicked the phone off and ran to the door of the room. The room was buzzing with nurses coming in and out. Charlie's friends were still by her side but whispering to one another. Their whispers combined made the room seem loud and busier. Charlie's eyes were still closed, but she appeared comforted, with her mother by her side holding her hand.

Stacy looked at James as he ran by her and yelled after him, "Where are you going?" She asked.

James' only response was "Police."

Aaron felt a ping of guilt for Sam. Sam had been here day and night. He should have been the one here when she woke. But Sam was nowhere to be found. They didn't know where he had run off to. Aaron was concerned Sam stumbled on his path to sobriety. Aaron hoped that wasn't the case. He couldn't imagine where Sam could be. He hoped he hadn't done anything rash.
Stacy left the room with Aaron's phone to call Sam. Aaron and Charlie's mother were at Charlie's side, trying to help lead her to consciousness.

Rage of Passion

Sam, still sitting in his truck, watched the sunrise behind him through his rearview mirror. He thought if all images in hindsight were as beautiful as that sunset through the rear mirror, life would be so much more perfect. Nearly 20 minutes later, the door to the house he'd been spying on all night opened. A bearded red-headed man emerged in boxers. His face was nearly healed, but faded bruises were visible, even to Sam, who was still sitting across the street in his truck. A renewed sense of anger formed in Sam's belly and burned through his body. He stepped out of the truck, put the 38 in his jeans' waistband, and then covered it with his tee-shirt.

The red-headed man began to walk to the back of his house. Sam watched him momentarily and then shut the truck door quietly and started to walk across the street towards the house. Sam walked casually as he always did, but he was strangely aware of everything. He could feel his pants rub his leg with every step he took. He could hear the scuff of his old work boots on the pavement, his comfortable tee shirt seems tight around his shoulders and arms now, and the weight of the gun in his waistband seemed to weigh a 100 pounds.
Sam stepped on the curb in front of the house. He walked boldly down the driveway leading to the backyard as if he belonged there. He rounded the corner of the house and found the red-headed man in boxers, smoking a cigarette and winding up a water hose.

The man looked at Sam, but Sam didn't speak. He just stared at the half-naked man. Finally, Sam asked, "John Butler?"

The man stood upright and answered, "Yeah."

Sam walked closer, still not speaking. He placed his hand on the gun but didn't pull it out yet. Sam looked to the ground, and when he looked up, Sam had a wicked smile on his face.

The man said, "I don't know what you want, but you aren't welcome here, so leave." The man seemed nervous by Sam's presence.

Sam didn't move, just stood there wickedly smiling. Sam reached behind his back, pulled the 38 from his pants, and held it down to his side.

Sam Said, "Charlie wanted me to come by."

"Who the hell is Charlie?" the man said. His nervous eyes gave him away. He knew exactly who Charlie was.

Sam aimed and held the gun on John Butler, not hesitating but reveling at the moment. Just then, he felt the phone in his pocket vibrate. Still holding the gun on Butler, he reached into his pants and pulled the phone out to see Aaron's name on the screen.

Sam flipped the phone open and said, "I'm busy right now."

Stacy said, "Sam, I'm on Aaron's phone; you need to come to the hospital."

Sam flatly asked, "Why?"

Stacy said, "It's Charlie. She is waking up. You should be here for this."

Sam's stomach bounced with relief but calmly ensured his face did not reflect any emotion.

Sam asked, "Has she been able to confirm John Butler yet."

Stacy said, "I don't see how that is important right now, but yes, she did. James got it on video."

It was then Sam began to hear very faint sirens in the distance. He stood there holding the gun on Butler. Butler was astonished at what was happening. His body language said it all. Butler's face was unreadable. He was trying to think of a move but wasn't sure what that move should be.

Stacy said, "Sam, where are you? Are those sirens in the background?"

The sirens were closing in, and Sam was conflicted now. What would Charlie want him to do.

Stacy, still waiting for an answer, began to get nervous as she could hear the sirens more vividly now. "Sam, I don't know where you are or what you are doing, but you need to get out of there now!"

Stacy may not have known where Sam was, but she had a pretty good idea of precisely what he was doing. She didn't want him to make the biggest mistake of his life.

Sam flipped the phone closed and, without another word to Butler, turned and walked away. He returned to his truck and watched as the police took Butler into custody.

Hospital

Charlie's mother was at the nursing station talking to the staff and waiting for Charlie's father to arrive at the hospital with Ryan. Stacy had gone in to talk to Charlie but had become so overwhelmed with emotion she had to step out for a moment. Aaron was still in the room. She was gently talking to her and expressing how grateful they all were to have her back. He'd told her Sam most of the time, all the guys had been there with Stacy, and they were all coming back as soon as they could.

He said, "But Sam was here the most. He sat with you day and night. He insisted on being the one to stay."

Charlie looked at Aaron strangely and mouthed the word 'really.' Aaron nodded yes but told her to save her strength.

Aaron said, "As much time as Sam spent here, I wish he was here when you woke up."

Charlie cocked her lip to one side and tried to shrug her shoulders.

Aaron said, "You don't have to tell me anything, just know, I didn't realize how close you two were."

Charlie looked at Aaron with wide eyes.

Aaron followed up by saying, "I don't know anything that happened and don't want to. I'm just glad he was there for you when we couldn't be."

Charlie squeezed her eyes shut and said, "I've missed him." Although her words were barely audible, they held the weight of the room. Aaron squeezed her hand.

The door opened, and Charlie's father appeared in the doorway with Ryan. Charlie's face lit up, her eyes widened, and she tried to smile. No words would have expressed the emotion in the room at that moment. Charlie took Ryan in her arms and squeezed him so fiercely, and for once, Ryan let her. He crawled up into the bed with her and laid next to her. His little face turned up to hers. He said, "I never ever want to be gone from you again."

Charlie smiled at him and nodded a firm nod of affirmation.

Reflection

James came into the room and called Charlie's parents out to the hall, explaining that John Butler had been arrested. He explained the case was very strong with the evidence the police had. However, they wanted a statement on record from Charlie to seal the case up.

James said, "As an officer of the court, I can take the statement on video. How do you think she will react to me asking her?"

Charlie's mother and father looked at each other and then to the floor in contemplation.

Finally, her father, who had always been a man of few words, said, "Just ask her, if she is reluctant, I'll talk to her. She needs to do this to keep that monster in jail."

Charlie's parents and James returned to Charlie's room and asked everyone to clear out. James started slowly and gently with Charlie. He explained the situation. Without hesitation, Charlie agreed.

James pulled out his cell phone and began to record, saying, "Ok, Charlie, take your time, try to be detailed and just tell us in your own words what happened."

Charlie looked to the camera and asked James, "Where do I start?"

"As close to the beginning as you are comfortable with," James replied.

Charlie inhaled deep and held it for a minute. She took a sip of water and then began, "I'd met Johnny on a website that, I thought it was for grief support, but it was more of a dating match site. It was nice to talk to men that had lost someone close to them, so, even though I realized, almost right away, that it was more of a dating website, I stayed on there."

Charlie paused for a minute, collecting her thoughts, then swallowed hard and continued, "A few months after I met Johnny or Redmen, was his screen name, we talked on the messenger part of Chatters for a while, maybe 3 or 4 months. He kept asking to meet me in person, but I wasn't ready for that. Finally, I agreed to meet him. I gave him my phone number, and we texted back and forth several weeks, then we met up at the coffee shop one afternoon." Again Charlie paused, but this time, she was reflecting on the meeting.

Charlie started again slowly, "The meeting with Johnny was normal. I actually enjoyed the conversation and company. We continued to text, and we met a few more times. I really started to like him, so he started to come out to the house and, mistakenly, I introduced him to Ryan. I didn't know how much of a mistake it was at the time, but it felt nice to have a male around the house again. I didn't think it was a match for a long-term commitment or anything, and I told him that a couple of times. I considered him a friend."

Charlie looked to James. He smiled as if to say continue. So, Charlie did, "Johnny came out to the house a couple of times a week for the next two months, and then I started noticing little things." Charlie was about to continue when James stopped her.

"Can you explain a little about what you noticed," James asked?

Charlie nodded and said, "Oh, ok. Well, I noticed little things like Ryan was disconnecting with him. I also noticed when he and Ryan were in a room alone, I'd walk in, and they would be holding my phone. When I'd ask what they were talking about, Ryan always said John wanted your phone. Also, he would question me about where I had been when he called. He got angry when I teased him about small things. What got to me most and what caused me to stop contacting him was he asked me to let him see my phone. There was nothing on my phone, but I didn't feel I should have to show him my phone. I thought I'd been clear, but I guess he didn't see it that way."

 James nodded to Charlie to continue. Charlie nodded back and said, "I mean, it was my phone, and I literally did nothing wrong. I owed him nothing. I guess me saying no made him mad, and he just lost his mind. He yelled at me, accused me of cheating, and just acted like an all-around jackass. So, I told him to get out and lose my number. I didn't hear from him for like two days, and then he started texting and calling me. At first, I replied to his text and answered his calls. After a while, it just got to be too much for me. I told him to stop, and he didn't, so I got a new number and phone. I mean, I couldn't move; I owned the house. Ryan was born here. It's all he's known, but I did what I could."

Charlie paused and took a sip of water but started right back in, "It had been a couple of months since I'd heard anything from him. I was actually starting to be comfortable and think maybe he had finally moved on. However, that wasn't the case. I started to receive letters in the mail. They weren't pleasant. I didn't keep the first few, but I started to keep them when they really got gross. They are hidden in my closet if the police need them. Anyway, I realized I was getting the letter because he didn't have my new cell phone. I looked on the Chatters application. He had sent me messages on there before he sent the letters, and when I didn't answer the messages, he started the letters. I messaged him on Chatters and told him to stop with the letters."

Charlie's eyes started to tear a little. "He stopped with the letters but started sending me packages. He sent small things at first, weird things like sugar packets and a box full of ladybugs. Then, the items got bigger. He sent a bunch of dead flowers and even a pair of his underwear. Which I thought was odd since we had not been in a sexual relationship." Charlie said shyly, glancing at her Father. Her father was looking at the floor and shaking his head.

James asked, "Was he ever violent with you?"

Charlie shook her head and said, "No, not at that point, but when I wasn't responding to anything he was doing, I guess he started getting mad. I saw him at the coffee shop one afternoon. He tried to speak to me, and I wouldn't respond to him. He kept raising his voice; I was getting so embarrassed. He threw his coffee off the table at me. I walked out, and he followed me and tried to pull me in that alley between the coffee shop and the bookstore."

Charlie wiped a tear off her cheek. Charlie's mother walked to her bedside and took her hand. Charlie continued, "James walked down the street and saw me. I was so thankful, but when I turned around, Johnny was gone. I just let it go because I was embarrassed and didn't want James to know." She finished and smiled slightly at James standing behind the camera.

"I don't know what happened after that. I don't know if he got scared or was reflecting on his actions, which I doubt, but I didn't hear from him again until the night he showed up at my house." Charlie said.

Charlie's eyes immediately saddened at the thought of that night. She looked to James then to her mother. Her mother smiled at her and squeezed her hand. Charlie continued, and the more she spoke, the more upset she became.

"I wasn't scared at first. I just didn't want to talk or see him. I mean, he looked bad." Charlie explained.

James asked, "What do you mean bad."

"He looked messy. His hair was messy, his clothes seemed dirty, and the oddest thing, he didn't have shoes on. Like he was at home that night and just grabbed his keys and drove out to my house in a hurry. I thought maybe he was drinking or something. Honestly, I was asleep when he showed up. I really wasn't thinking clearly. I did tell him to leave when I cracked the door. But he pushed the door open, and it smacked me right in the face and knocked me down. I heard him put my baby in his room, but I couldn't do anything to stop him. I was trying to recover from being hit in the face. When he returned, I tried to reach my gun, but it was gone." Charlie said, sniffing.

James said, "They found the gun. It was in his house."

Charlie continued, "Anyway, I realized I had to do something because Ryan was in the other room. I just wanted to protect Ryan. So, I fought back as much as I could. I elbowed him in the nose and scratched his arms, but after that, I think I just pissed him off because I don't remember what happened." Charlie finished.

James said, "Apparently, you got some kicks in. You punched him and broke his nose. You did some damage, girl."

Charlie's father handed her a tissue and walked out of the room. He was visibly upset. James clicked off the phone. "I'm going to submit this video to the police now. I don't want to take any chances."

James leaned over and kissed Charlie on the forehead, "I'm sorry I had to ask you to do that." He said.

Charlie smiled a weak smile, "It's ok, it had to be done. So, I really kicked his ass, huh?"

James nodded and smiled, "Yeah, you sure did."

Hospital-Sam

After the video was complete, Charlie wanted to see Ryan more. Charlie's Mother brought Ryan into the room. They were lying together in Charlie's bed alone. Finally, everything had settled down momentarily. Mother and son enjoyed some one-on-one time when the door opened, and Sam peeked around the door. Ryan looked at him curiously, then looked to his mom. Charlie said in a whisper, "It's alright, baby, go find grandpa and get a snack, then come back for more cuddles."

Ryan did as he was told, although hesitantly. He didn't know this man that had appeared in her room. With a little more reassurance from Charlie, Ryan left to find his grandfather.

When Ryan left, Sam came into the room and took a seat next to Charlie's bed. Charlie put her hand out to Sam, and he took it.

Charlie Said, "Where have you been?"

Sam sheepishly looked down and shook his head, "Just taking care of business."

Charlie smiled at him, her voice still rough. She said, "You look really good."

Sam smiled and laughed a silent laugh, "I know, thanks. You my, beauty, are looking a little rough around the edges."

Charlie laughed as big as she could without hurting her still sore ribs. People came in and out of the room, but Sam stayed the entire time. He had heard Ryan's first words to his mother were, 'I never ever want to leave you again.' Sam was feeling that way right now and could understand how Ryan felt. Before visiting, hours were over, and Charlie's parents took Ryan back to their place. Charlie asked Ryan to come to meet Sam. When Ryan walked in, he looked at Sam very curiously.

Ryan was a polite child, and when Charlie introduced the two, Ryan said, "Nice to meet you." And put his hand out to shake Sam's, Sam returned the gesture. Ryan seemed to want to like Sam right away but was hesitant. Sam told Ryan thank you, and Ryan told Sam your welcome, then asked why Sam was thanking him. Sam said, "Because you are a hero. You saved your mother's life. I also hear you were a big help in finding out who hurt her. So that makes you a hero also." Ryan smiled at Sam and told Sam, "Well then, thank you for staying and babysitting my mom when I couldn't stay here."

Sam smiled and held in a giggle and told Ryan, your welcome. Sam, Ryan, and Charlie stayed in the room together, coloring and watching cartoons until Charlie's parents came in and said it was time to get Ryan to bed. Charlie kissed him fiercely and told him she would see him tomorrow. Sam stayed with Charlie through the night. He continued to stay for three more nights, and the doctors were talking about releasing Charlie.

The guys had met with Sam earlier on that third day and asked Sam if he thought Charlie was strong enough now to answer questions about Lock. Sam wasn't sure, but he told them he'd feel her out and let them know. That night Charlie had turned to her side in the hospital bed to talk to Sam and fallen into a deep sleep. Sam laid his head back and drifted to sleep in the recliner chair in Charlie's room. He was awakened by Charlie screaming, and she was upright in the bed. Sam rushed to her side and held her close as she settled her breathing.

Charlie said, "I had a nightmare."

Sam kissed her forehead, "Do you want to talk about it?" he asked her.

"No, not yet. I know I will have to some time but not yet." She said, resting in his arms.

Sam kicked his boots off, got into bed next to her, and held her close against his chest.

"Can I ask you something that may be hard for you to answer?" He said.

"Yes," She answered hesitantly. She assumed he would ask her about John Butler and how it had all happened.

Sam considered his following words carefully. He inhaled deep and then released it, saying, "Well, I never asked before, but I feel like we are in a different place now. I just want you to tell me the truth."

She looked up at him and said, "I've never lied to you."

Sam corrected his previous statement, "No, I know that. Ok, this is coming out wrong." He said and tried to start over. "I think I know what happened in Florida before I came to pick you up," Sam said.

Charlie was surprised by the question. She was taken entirely off guard. She started to interrupt, and Sam stopped her, and he continued, "If Lock raped you, it would never change the way I feel about Ryan. I will accept him as your son and only your son."

Charlie grew very still, with her face in Sam's chest and their arms around one another.

Sam asked, "Charlie, is that what happened?"

Charlie began to cry, and Sam's heart broke for her. "Sweetheart, it's ok," Sam said, trying to comfort her.

Charlie always knew she would one day have to explain to Sam what had happened those few weeks in Florida. After all, he'd dropped everything to come after her. He deserved to know. In all the ways she had imagined telling him, this strange situation never entered her mind. She could have never prepared herself for this.

Charlie looked to Sam, "No, that isn't what happened." Sam, confused by her answer, waited for her to continue.

"I went to see Lock in Florida after the funeral. I got in his car and threatened to expose him. See, I knew that he'd seen Rylan and that he knew she was there. All I needed was evidence of that. So, when I got into his car, I pocketed his cell phone. I cloned it." Charlie said, wiping her eyes and nose. "I guess he figured out it was me that had the phone, so he came looking for it, but I had already dropped it in the mail to him. Anonymously, of course. As far as I know, he didn't know I took it." She turned to lay on her back and continued, "He scared me when he showed up at the hotel. At this point, I knew he'd killed Rylan, and when he showed up at the hotel, he looked crazed. He said he'd be back, and he was going to hunt me down like the bitch and kill me. So that's when I called you."

Sam asked what proof she'd gotten that confirmed he'd done it.

Charlie said, "I have this old phone, and a picture of Stacy and me is on the phone. It's encrypted. If you click the photo, it gives you a code. Then you take my new phone and enter the code into the same picture on my new phone, and the evidence will pop up. It's a picture of Rylan in Florida from Lock's phone. The IP address from the picture will prove that he knew she was there. He'd been stalking her for months before he found her outside in that alley."

The guys had shown Sam the picture and mentioned it was strange of her to have it saved. Her explanation made sense to Sam.

Sam said, "Charlie, you know you have to turn this information in. Why haven't you."

Charlie sat silent for a moment, "Do you know how hard it has been for me to look at my beautiful son every day and call his name, knowing he's named for Rylan and I know who killed her? But I am scared. I have to protect him at all costs. I held on to the information and planned to turn it in. I was waiting till he and I were more stable."

Sam ran his hand through her hair, "You don't have to worry anymore. As long as you will have me, I will be right by your side. I'm not going anywhere."

"Sam?" Charlie said almost shyly, "Ryan, is your son."

Sam's heart stopped, his breath stopped, and his eyes clouded over, "He's not your husband's son," Sam said questioningly.

"No. I let people believe that because I didn't know how you would react. I didn't know if we were ever going to resolve this between us. You became so distant, and you started your own path when we got home. I just couldn't tell you." Charlie said, tears running down her face, "Please don't be angry, and I'm so, so sorry you thought I was hurt, and Ryan was Lock's." She finished.

Sam's body started to function again, "I'm not angry. You were right. I would have been a terrible father back then. I'm just now gaining the trust of my other son."

Charlie smiled. "I'm so glad he's your son. You're a good man Sam."

Trial

Charlie's hair was pulled back into a tight bun at the nape of her neck. She sat next to Sam in the courtroom, dressed in a silk white dress shirt, Linen Kahiki skirt that fell mid-calf and brown heels. Sam sat with her on the second row wearing his one pair of Kahiki pants and a brand new white tee-shirt, which, to dress up the outfit, he tucked in and put a belt on. They sat silently as forensic specialists were giving testimony in John Butler's trial. For a moment, Charlie and Sam looked at each other. Sam looked down into Charlie's face and gave her a little wink. Sam had been an incredible help since Charlie had been released from the hospital.

Charlie had gone to stay with Sam in his home. She loved her house but couldn't bring herself to return. She sold the home, and Sam asked Charlie to stay with him indefinitely. At first, Charlie wasn't sure. She felt almost as if she had invaded his life since she left the hospital. However, when Sam dropped on his knee and asked her to marry him, Charlie realized there was no place she wanted to be other than right there with Sam. She realized she was a welcome invasion for Sam.

As Charlie sat in the courtroom now, trying to listen to the experts drone on about quarter size this and that, she kept zoning out. She didn't want to be in the courtroom anymore. She and Sam had been there for the first part of the trial. She had testified. She thought the prosecutor had done a great job and had no doubt that Butler would be convicted. Through the police investigation, Charlie learned that Butler had been drinking and been involved in some heavy drug use in the months prior to the attack. He had a history of stalking women and a history of domestic violence. In fact, Charlie learned that he had gotten up that night, unable to sleep, gotten dressed, and drove out to Charlie's house. He'd been smoking meth on the way out. The prosecution pointed out that he probably didn't even realize he hadn't combed his hair or forgot to put shoes on.

Charlie's mind flashed back to Sam's back deck a few nights before. The guys had come over to celebrate Sam and Charlie's engagement. They cooked steaks on the grill, and everyone had brought delicious food. Charlie was delighted to see Stacy and Aaron making a go of a relationship again.

After the food was eaten, and most all the stories had been told that needed to be said, Charlie and the faithful five, plus Stacy, were all sitting quietly, basking in the cool of the evening. Everyone had some kind of beverage in their hands. Stacy and Aaron were whispering to themselves. Vin's wife, Ella, was on her way from the city. They planned to spend the weekend with Aaron and Stacy. Sam looked at Charlie and asked if she was alright. Charlie snuggled up to Sam. She put her head under his chin.

"I feel so complete. How could either of us ask for anything more than this." She said, waving her hand out over the deck. Sam kissed her on the top of her head, pulled her in close, and squeezed her tight.

"I love you, Charlie Rae," Sam Said

"I love you too, Sam," Charlie said

As Charlie's mind returned to the present, Sam put his hand on her leg and gave it a little squeeze. He mouthed the words, "Are you alright."

Charlie smiled and nodded, yes, that she was alright.

When the judge released the courtroom for the day, Charlie said, "Ryan is in the hall waiting for us."

They began to head slowly to the hall as everyone exited the courtroom like cattle. Sam stopped and looked at Charlie, "I've been thinking about something all day." Sam said.

"Oh yeah, what's that?" Charlie asked, looking up at him with her big blue eyes.

"I know where we could get married right here, right now, today," Sam said with a smile as big as his face could hold.

Charlie laughed, "What? Are you kidding?", She replied.

Sam said, "No, let's get Ryan, go over to the judge and get married. Then we can spend the next three weeks on the beach. You know, like we did all those years ago."

Charlie, with an uncertain smile on her face, looked around in all directions. Then dropped her focus directly on Sam. "Alright. Let's do it. Let's get Ryan and get married. Can we leave tomorrow for the beach?" She asked, hoping he'd say yes so they didn't have to sit through the rest of the trial.

Sam laughed, "Of course, I can't take another day of this."

They grabbed hands and pushed their way out the courtroom door to find Ryan with Charlie's mother.

After their nuptials, Charlie, Sam, and Ryan loaded into Sam's Truck. They drove out of Harriston and into the sunset. No one looked back to Harriston that day, and no one looked back from that day forward.